FINDING FRIENDS

THE REUNION OF A LIFETIME

CAROLYN KEMP

Dedication

This book is for Carolyn and Adam, my constant source of support. I love you both dearly with all my heart.

I also thank my friends and family for their help through a very difficult period in my life. This book is a product of this time, and its production is testament to the support you have all shown to me.

This book is Copyright 2019 Carolyn Kemp

All rights reserved. No part of this publication may be reproduced, stored in any retrieval system, or transmitted, in any form or by any means, electronic, mechanical, photocopying, recording or otherwise, without the prior written permission of the author or publishers.

This book is a work of fiction. Names, characters, businesses, organisations, places and events other than those clearly in the public domain, are either the product of the author's imagination or are used ficticiously. Any resemblance to actual persons, living or dead, events or locales is entirely coincidental.

CONTENTS

Title Page	1
Dedication	3
Copyright	4
Chapter 1 - The Reunion	7
Chapter 2 - James' Night	10
Chapter 3 - Hannah's Dilemma	13
Chatper 4 - Building Confidence	18
Chapter 5 - Friends and Conflict	22
Chapter 6 - Old Friends	26
Chapter 7 - The Dancefloor	31
Chapter 8 - The Morning After	36
Chapter 9 - Returning Home	39
Chapter 10 - Call On A Friend	45
Chapter 11 - Clearing Out	54
Chapter 12 - Monday Morning	58
Chapter 13 - A Night In The Pub	65
Chapter 14 - Shell Shock	73
Chapter 15 - Recovery and Discovery	81
Chapter 16 - Night And Day	92
Chapter 17 - The Other Woman	111
Chapter 18 - Making A Statement	123

Chapter 19 - Investigations and Discoveries	137
Chapter 20 - Date Night	145
Chapter 21 - Looking Back And Making Plans	154
Chapter 22 - Evenings In And Out	164
Chapter 23 - The Grand Plan	173
Chapter 24 - A Fun Day Out	178
Chapter 25 - An Evening Together	194
Chapter 26 - Putting Plans In Motion	200
Chapter 27 - A Question Of Trust	206
Chapter 28 - True Friends	212
Chapter 29 - What The Future Holds	215
About The Author	218

CHAPTER 1

The Reunion

The ballroom was an overwhelming sight. The most beautiful room that Hannah had ever seen. It was going to be a perfect evening, with her new fiance by her side, she was going to show them all just how far she'd come since she'd left school.

No expense appeared to have been spared on the 25th anniversary reunion of the class of 1994. Around the exquisitely dressed room hung pictures of the class mates throughout school. Some gathered by parents and loved ones included pictures of kids on their first day at secondary school in new uniform, those big group pictures from drama presentations and of course the obligatory sports day pictures. Other pictures supplied by the school included class photos through the years, pictures from assemblies and award ceremonies.

Whilst it was usually the school who would organise the reunions, these would normally be a disco in the old school hall with a row of trestle tables covered in snacks and drinks, but this year was different. James Richardson had funded the whole thing and arranged the ballroom and entertainment. It was his way of "giving a little something back" to his former classmates. He agreed that the school could still provide food, if only to keep the old headmistress Mrs. Morris happy who had made it quite clear that the school should at least supply something for the evening.

James was never the sports guy, never excelled at maths or

english, he was a "C" student, middle of the road right across the board. He didn't get together with the popular groups, he didn't have any real friends, he was picked on once or twice but generally left alone. Mostly people would say "Hi" to him in the corridor, everyone knew him and to James that was fine. The fact was that James was happy not having to worry about friends. Having friends would mean having to care about their opinions or needing to be there when they needed a friend to talk to. James had a fine life on his own.

It hadn't always been that way of course, before they went to secondary school James had Hannah. Hannah was his best friend in the whole world. Hannah's family lived four doors down on the same side of the same street. James and Hannah were born within a month of each other and their mothers had bumped into each other at baby groups when they were less than a year old. So had begun the ritual of mothers meeting up most days and James and Hannah playing together throughout their childhood. They went to the same places, started playgroup at the same time and were even in the same class at primary school.

It all started to change shortly after Hannah's 11th birthday. One morning before school, Hannah was talking to her new friend Claire.

"My mum said you could come over for Tea tomorrow after school", said Claire
"Oh, I've already arranged to meet James after school tomorrow, we're working on our project together", replied Hannah
"I don't know why you hang around with him, it's not like you have anything in common"
"Don't be stupid, we have lots in common"
"Other than living on the same street and occasionally liking the same TV programmes?"
"If that's the case, what do we have in common? We don't even live on the same street"
"We understand each other, we talk about things. I knew about

your crush on that Paperboy in the shop who moved away, you never could have discussed that with James"

Claire was right, James had never listened to her, not when it counted. James and Hannah were just two kids who'd grown up playing games together and they'd never really developed beyond that.

Claire started hanging around with Hannah more. Their conversations developed, no longer were they talking of toys, games and TV programmes (although these still did come up in conversation). They began discussing different clothes, when they'd be allowed to wear makeup and even what they thought of different boys, which ones would like cute as they got older, which ones would be the strong sporty ones and even which they think would be ideal husband material (although they normally agreed none of them!). During those last 3 months of primary school Hannah and Claire became the closest knit of friends.

James had noticed Hannah wasn't around as much, but hey she was hanging around with other girls, she had new friends. By the time the summer holiday came around, they hardly talked anymore.

CHAPTER 2

James' Night

James looked around the ballroom, this was going to be the best night. A chance to see all those faces from his teenage years. When school had finished, they'd all gone their separate ways, James had been offered an apprenticeship by his uncle's power company, and that was that. He'd moved 150 miles away and never looked back.

James's life would really change 13 years later, at the age of 29 when having worked his way up through the company to the position of Engineering Director, he awoke one day to the news that his uncle had passed away from a heart attack overnight and had left him as the major shareholder in the company.

Despite his professional success, he had continued to keep everyone distant. He was content to work during the day and at night enjoy watching sport and playing computer games. His world centered around his needs, and that was great. At least until the school announced the reunion.

The invite had arrived in the post at his parents' house. A single look at the invite and he was transported back, memories of all his classmates. He had developed, he was so much more confident now. He had money and he wanted people to know he had changed. He contacted the school and arranged to move the venue to one of his choosing. He set the wheels in motion and before he knew it, a week later he was booking a ballroom.

So here he was standing, looking at himself in a mirror in a private room at the grand ballroom. He suddenly started weighing up his physical appearance up, in his suit and tie and with his slight stubble and his strong jaw, he suddenly realised, he looked like a fairytale prince from a cartoon. He laughed at the thought and then took a deep breath and opened the door to the ballroom where guests were already arriving.

James crossed the floor and went to the bar and asked for a vodka and coke. The barman served it and went back to arranging the bottles so that the labels all faced outwards. James started his drink, leant up against the bar and surveyed the hall, the pictures everywhere, the DJ playing early 90s songs at a relatively low volume and the ten or so faces that he recognised along with their partners. He crossed the floor to the buffet, a number of people said hi to him as he walked, he smiled and replied with a nod and a smile. Somehow the faces seemed warm and familiar but all of their names seem to have escaped him. He got to the buffet and reviewed his options. The food was the standard school buffet, sandwiches, sausage rolls, vol-au-vents, cheese and pineapple, and chicken drumsticks. The only small concession that Mrs. Morris had made was that it wasn't going to all be on disposable trays and paper plates. So here was a basic buffet presented on fine china. He sighed at the selection, turned around and started looking at the pictures.

He was stood by pictures of the different classes at the start of secondary school. Each classes group photo complete with a list of names underneath and below that a comment panel for guests to write on. The comment panel had been James's idea. James wanted to see everyone again, but as his experience of school had been comparatively bland, he also wanted everyone else's memories of the time they had at school. Stood next to him in his first secondary school picture was Rob. Rob was the class joker, he'd tried hard to be friends with James, but James just didn't reciprocate the friendship.

James turned to his left and there was a collage of first day pictures taken by parents. A hundred pictures of children in uniform that was usually slightly to big for them. In the centre was the picture his mother had taken of him in September 1989 with his horrible side parting that he'd always hated. He'll never forget the look on his mother's face when he'd come home in the middle of summer 1994 with his hair having been nearly all shaved off. He had told her that he wanted to create his own identity, but really he just hated that hairstyle. Meanwhile on the other side of the room, in had walked Hannah and her fiance Paul.

CHAPTER 3

Hannah's Dilemma

Hannah spotted him across the ballroom. She knew it was him, she'd seen him on the news often enough, this was James, her friend James. He was the first boy she'd ever kissed (even if it was only for a dare). The sad truth was after that day with Claire, she'd hardly spoken to him, and never at secondary school. Within a year, birthday and christmas cards dried up. Their parents didn't even speak anymore. They were left in a situation where they barely acknowledged each other's existence. But, the truth was that looking back Hannah still held a special place in her heart for him. He was the closest thing she'd had as a brother growing up, and she'd let him slip away from her. Tonight this was all going to change, she was going to be that friend.

She asked Paul to go and get her a drink, she needed to do this next part alone. As she crossed the room, she felt her mouth getting dry and the slight panic starting to form in her head. Suddenly a million doubts were swimming through her head:

"What if he doesn't want to know me?"
"What if he doesn't remember our friendship the same?" and worse still
"What if he hates me?"

"*Get a grip*" she told herself "*It'll be fine, you'll be fine, just talk to him.*"

She walked over to the picture board where James was standing looking at the photos. She stood beside him and said the first thing that popped into her head as she looked forwards at the pictures

"I don't know why my mother insisted on giving me that bloody haircut"

James didn't even turn to look at her, he knew it was Hannah, he had felt her beside him and just knew. He just simply replied, "but you always took your hair down as soon as we got into school".

They both grinned to themselves and then slowly looked at each other.

"Hey Jimjam" said Hannah
"Hey Hannyhan" said James

In a moment the awkwardness between them was gone, James gave Hannah a big hug. Hannah hugged him right back, a moment she didn't want to end. "I've missed you", she whispered in his ear, tears starting to form.

James whispered back "I have so miss…"
"Oi! That's a little too friendly for my liking!" yelled Paul from across the room

Thankfully it was still early and few people were here, but everyone who was here was looking at Paul as he stormed across the floor. James and Hannah both still holding each other, looking sideways across at Paul.

"Not even 5 minutes here, and you're grinding up against some ex-boyfriend? Which one is this, Chris? Jason? Come on pal, speak up, who are you?"

"I'm James", James said calmly as him and Hannah let go of each other.

"James? You never said you'd dated a James at school!"

"I never dated James. He's different, he's special to me…can we take this conversation somewhere else?"
"Special! What does that mean?"
"Let's go somewhere else and talk about this calmly"
"Calm? Fuck off! You've kept this bloke, who doesn't look like he's short of a bit of cash, from me! I thought we told each other everything."
"We do, but it's complicated."
"Complicated how? Some secret love? Your actual date for this evening? You were going to dump me for him?"
"No, now shut up, come here and I'll explain everything"

James interjected and said "Come on, there is a room over here. You guys go and have a chat. And Han, let me know if you want me to come in"
Paul starts again "Han is it?!"
Hannah shuts him straight down "Fucking shut up, this is my school reunion, you want to know, I will tell you, just not in a shouting match in front of everyone. Now come in here".

With that, Hannah took Paul by the hand and pulled him into the room where James had been getting ready just a short while earlier.

Hannah closed the door behind them and sat on the chair next to a small round table. Paul continued to stand by the door.

"What the fuck is this all about?" said Paul
"Look, I don't know what you are thinking, but James is just a friend" replied Hannah
"He didn't look like just a friend"
"Okay, so he isn't just a friend. Its difficult to explain"
"I'll say, so are you fucking him or what?"
"Is that what you think of me?"
"You're the one who can't explain who the man of mystery is"
"It isn't anything like that. He's….he's special to me"
"Just tell me, is he a boyfriend?"

"No, he's…" Hannah was still struggling to find the right words to describe him "…he's James" was the best she could muster.
"What the fuck does that mean?!", Paul was holding the door handle, he wasn't getting anywhere, at this moment he really felt like telling Hannah the engagement was off and leaving, but he needed the answers to his questions.
"James…we grew up together. He was like a brother to me"
"You don't have a brother"
"I didn't say he was my brother, he was like a brother. I know I've never told you about him. By the time we got to secondary school, we weren't that close. Claire had convinced me to stop being friends with him when we were younger and we'd never seen eye to eye since then"
"I'm still not getting the brother thing"
"He lived down the road, we were the same age, both single children and our mums hung around together so we kind of looked out for each other when we were young"
"So, he's no threat to us"
"He isn't no." but in her heart, she knew that Paul's reaction and lack of trust meant that quite honestly, she was questioning whether she was with the right man.

She had been so sure when she'd walked in, she was going to make peace with James (already done), introduce Paul to everyone, catch up with people she hadn't seen for years and get details of people to invite to the wedding too! The problem was, in 30 seconds Paul had ruined it. He had totally overreacted at her hugging another man. It was clear that he didn't trust her.

Paul suddenly said "You never mentioned him, I need some time to take this in." and he turned to open the door. As he pushed the handle down, he looked over his shoulder and said, "I'm sorry". Within a moment he was gone and the door closed behind him.

Hannah sat there at the table, looking at her reflection in the mirror, *what had happened to her dream evening?*

In the hall, James had seen Paul leave the room and dart for the door. *There was a guy who needed to chill out* was all that James could think. He gave it 30 seconds in case Hannah was following, but no, the door stayed shut.

He walked to the door and knocked gently. "Han?", he could here sobbing from the other side.

CHATPER 4

Building Confidence

"Han?", James knocked again and this time opened the door slowly. There she was sat at the table in tears. James walked in and closed the door, he went and sat on the other chair. "Hey, what happened?", he started looking around her reddened face.

"Did he hit you?"
"No" she sobbed "he wouldn't ever."
James grabbed a tissue from the box on the side. He started to wipe her face.
"What happened? Do you want to tell me?"
"Paul happened" she burst into tears again
"Do you want to talk about it?" said James as he put his arm around her Slowly she calmed down, just feeling James holding her made her feel better.
"He overreacted, he knows he did, but he didn't know about you…us…our history. The real problem is, he's always been like it"
"What, an arsehole?"
"No, jealous, overprotective of his fianceé"
"Fianceé?"
"Yeah, we're supposed to be getting married."
"Wow, I never had you down for that. You always said marriage was stupid"
"The last time we spoke about things like that, I was ten. Any ten year old will say marriage is stupid."
"Yeah, but you were pretty insistent, as I recall, you punched

18

Tim for saying he'd marry you"
Hannah giggled a little, "yeah I did, but that was then"
"And you're a different person now?"
"Yes, I'm a woman, can't you tell?"
"Well, you haven't threatened to break my Action Man since I saw you, so definitely more mature than you were." James grinned and Hannah allowed herself to smile.

"Let's get your face sorted, you need to get out there and see people, and we can't have you looking a mess". James wiped the last of her tears and she looked in her handbag for her emergency makeup.
"I'll give you a few minutes, then I want to see you out there. If you are feeling fragile or need a friend, come and see me. I have no one with me, we can walk around together for a bit until you feel comfortable"

There is was, in a matter of minutes Hannah was suddenly back with her friend James, and just like always, together they could do anything. No one stood a chance when they were together as kids, and now they could take on the world as adults.

James wandered back out into the hall, a few faces looked across at him. No-one was going to dare say a word to him though. He went to the bar to get another drink, whilst the bartender was serving him, he took a few seconds to compose himself back to the position of confidence he'd been in earlier in the evening.

He'd got himself worked up over the last few weeks for tonight, the thoughts of who he wanted to see, who he hoped would be there, but the last few minutes had completely swept him away. Hannah just hadn't been a factor that he'd considered. He guessed he must have known that she'd be there, but any interaction with her hadn't been part of his plan. In that moment, a switch deep inside of him had been turned on. He needed to protect his friend and support her in her time of need.

He turned from the bar and looked back across the hall. Hannah was just closing the door to the side room, she looked uneasily around the room. James smiled and gave her a small wave from the bar. She walked over to him, feeling like all eyes in the place were on her. The truth was, everyone had gone back to conversing or dancing or looking at the pictures. She wasn't the centre of attention that she felt at the time.

As she got to the bar, James said "What do you want? Rum and Coke?"
"Do you really think I should be drinking?" said Hannah
"Why? Do you have a reason not to?"
"Emotional wreck of a woman and alcohol, it could all end in tears"
"No...the evening started with tears, the point is to improve the evening, and make you feel like it was a good idea to come here. Now do you want a drink?"
"Okay, yes a rum and coke sounds good." Hannah finally relented "Anyway, it was a good idea. I got to see you, and we're talking for the first time in what? 30 years?".

James turned to the barman and ordered the drink.

James's mind started overthinking the situation, as always and suddenly he said "Of course, if you hadn't spoken to me, if we hadn't of hugged, maybe the evening wouldn't have started in tears"
"Don't let's talk about that. I'd rather we didn't mention that idiot Fianceé of mine. He'll be alright once he calms down and actually thinks about things"

James took a swig of his drink.

"Okay, let's start this properly, start how these things are supposed to go" said James.
"How's that then?"
James put on a mock big smile and started in an enthusiastic voice "Oh! Hi Hannah, you are looking fabulous. What have you done with yourself since school? Have you a family or kids?

The Reunion Of A Lifetime

Where are you living?" James carried on his one sided conversation "Oh me? I'm doing very well for myself. Yes, a millionaire didn't you know? Oh you know, never found time for a family or the right woman."

Hannah found herself grinning inanely at James's mock conversation.

"Is that really how these things are supposed to be?" she said.
"I don't know, but it is how the movies always portray them" he responded
"I'm amazed at you"
"What that I'm so fabulous?"
"No, that you still think you're funny."
"I don't think I'm funny, I know I'm funny. People tell me that all the time"
"You have a fortune, people tell you what you want to hear"
"Really, and you're different are you?"
"Absolutely, I know you don't know the difference between funny and cringeworthy"
"Maybe I do, maybe I'm just playing stupid"
"There's no need to play"

Hannah surprised herself, she was enjoying the light-hearted banter with James. It really was like having her long lost brother back.

More people by now had started to come in and everyone was starting to mingle around. It was time to officially start the evening.

"I need to go and announce the evening" he said to Hannah
"You're going to leave me to go and get on stage?" she said
"Only for a moment, unless you want to come up there with me?" *"Where had that come from?"* he suddenly thought.
"Okay then." Hannah found herself saying, inside she suddenly thought *"What am I doing? I hate being centre of attention."*
"Let's get this started then"

CHAPTER 5

Friends and Conflict

James took Hannah's hand and led her up the steps onto the stage, they walked together to the DJ booth and James grabbed the microphone. He squeezed Hannah's hand and nodded at the DJ, the music was turned down.

"I just thought I'd better say something to start this evening off." He began "I had planned a speech, but no one wants to hear me talk for ages, plus I've forgotten most of it anyway. Look, I'd like to welcome you all, hope everyone has fun and gets to catch up with old friends. Food is over there, bar is over there, now let's get some music on and start this party properly!"

The DJ hit play and suddenly "Wake me up before you go-go" was blaring out of the sound system. James realised had been holding Hannah's hand whilst announcing, he began to let go of her hand.

"No, not yet, let's get off the stage first" she said.

James squeezed her hand again. "Of course" he said and guided her back down the steps to the bar area once again.

Once by the bar, he let go of her hand. "Sorry, I didn't mean to hold your hand up there" he said
"No, it was fine, it made me feel safe"
"Now we've probably got a room full of people who think we're a couple"
"No, at least ten of them saw us earlier"

"They saw your fianceé accuse you of having an affair with me"
"Oh fuck, yeah, so probably"
"Anyway, you know what rumours were like when we were at school. They wouldn't let a little thing like the truth get in the way of a good story now, would they?"
Hannah smiled again, "I guess you're right"

For the next hour or so, they propped up the bar chatting to people as they ordered drinks exchanging "Hi, how are you doing?" with everyone. No-one asked if they were a couple and they didn't say anything either way, it was just like little pockets of people chatting together.

After a while, out of Hannah's view, Claire approached the bar.

"I knew you'd run back to him eventually" said Claire
Hannah spun around, her head already starting on defense before she opened her mouth "What did you say?"
"I knew you'd go back to him, once you didn't have me to help you."
Hannah's anger was already boiling up inside her, after just two sentences from Claire.
"Of course you did, because you were always right weren't you?"
"Well I kept you on the right track through school, didn't I? Imagine how big a loser you could have been if you'd hung around with him through school."
"Okay, that's enough. I don't know who you think you are or what gives you the right to be like that, but I am not the same kid I once was"
"Oh really? I made you what you are today!"
"No, you really didn't. All you did was make me miserable"
"Miserable... I suppose that's one way to describe you"
"Woah ladies, let's calm this down" said James
"Anyway, did you get with him before he got given the money or after?" said Claire
"Now that's a really interesting question" said Paul
"Paul? when did you come back?" said Hannah

"I've been sat over there for a while, watching you and the 'brother' chatting and laughing with people without a care in the world" said Paul
"Claire, this is"
"Paul, trust me, we've already met"
"Okay, so of all the people you should happen to talk to, you spoke to my fianceé"
"Oh, Paul's your fianceé, I thought you and peachy were together." Claire had always called James peachy, something to do with a book they read at primary school. "Anyway, Paul and me, we were at uni together. We knew each other very well, if you know what I mean"

Hannah's head couldn't comprehend this. The girl who'd pushed her away from James, the girl who was always the popular one, that she'd hung around with and lived in the shadow of at school, was also the Claire who broke her fianceé's heart at uni by sleeping with his best mate whilst he was at his father's funeral? Why did it have to be her?

"Paul?" said Hannah
"I went out for some air, and bumped into Claire. I know I said I'd never forgive her and would kill her if I ever saw her again, but in that moment she'd listened to me."

Claire had an evil smile starting to form on the side of her lips. She was in control of this situation. She held all of the cards and it was making Hannah squirm. She'd forgotten how much fun this could be, to hold someone's emotions in the palm of your hand.

"So," started Claire "one thing led to another and I convinced him to come back in with me." A full cheshire cat grin was now on Claire's face. Hannah turned away and looked at James who had been watching this conversation unfold. Hannah's fists were clenched, James knew what she was thinking. He looked Hannah straight in the eyes and mouthed "Don't, she isn't worth it".

Hannah knew he was right, but she also knew how satisfying it would be to smack her in the mouth. She took a deep breath, slowly she unclenched her fists. "See," said Claire "he's right, violence isn't the answer" and with that Hannah spun around and slapped Claire full across the left cheek, a slap so hard it echoed around the room. "Don't you dare tell me what to do." she said "I haven't been told what I can and can't do since I left school, and don't think you can start again now"

CHAPTER 6

Old Friends

A round of applause echoed around the room as classmate of old cheered on Hannah. Over the applause someone yelled "I didn't know you had it in you!". Claire looked around the room, she suddenly realised no-one here was on her side. As her face reddened, not just from the slap but the embarrassment of having been shown up. She turned and made for the door. Paul looked at Hannah, shook his head in a disapproving manner and ran after Claire.

"OK everyone.", said Hannah, "Now I've made it clear that I'm not to be messed with, can we all carry on having a good time?"

A faint murmer of agreement was made by the onlookers and people began going about their business.

"Do you feel better for that?" said James
"You know I do" replied Hannah smiling
"Had you planned to do it?"
"No, I was going to steer clear of her tonight, but she came straight for me. Anyway, if I'd really planned anything, it would have had to involve some sort of drawn out torture."
"Ooo, nasty. So what was the deal with you and Claire anyway?"
"I thought she was my friend when we were at school. It is only since I left school and looked back at my time there that I realised that she was just a controlling bitch through school. Keeping me down just enough so that I couldn't rise above her, whilst she took all the credit. I can't believe that her and Paul had been

together, it makes my stomach turn just to think about it."
"It is one hell of a coincidence, isn't it?"

Just then a woman's voice came from behind him, "James?". He spun around to see who it was, and there he was greeted by Karen standing not 2 feet behind him.

He had secretly hoped that Karen was going to come. Karen Jennings, the girl he'd noticed when she joined his class at the age of 14. She was different, not someone who'd known him forever, but she didn't even acknowledge him. This to him had made her mesmerising, he wanted to know her, he wanted to talk to her, he wanted to spend time with her. She was his one and only crush. He didn't know what to do about it, he didn't have the confidence or want to risk getting hurt. So he'd continued to watch her, dream about the life they could have, but never approached her.

The truth was the ballroom was entirely for Karen's benefit. If he could meet her, he might be able to finally tell Karen exactly how he'd felt. But, if he was going to do this, he was going to do it his way. He needed the right environment, that is what had led to him to rearrange the whole evening in the first place.

The problem was, he had wanted Karen to be there before, but it was all wrong now. He was supporting Hannah, she was his focus, his true friend that hadn't given up on him. Well this coupled with the fact that there was also the tiny problem that he clammed up whenever Karen had spoken to him in the past.

"Um...err...Hi" James managed to stutter out
"Are you OK James?" said Karen
"...I'm fine, just a bit flustered" James eventually said
"Oh, busy night?" asked Karen
"You could say that" said Hannah
"Hannah! How are you?" said Karen. James saw his opportunity to step back whilst Hannah and Karen began to talk, he started to turn away when Hannah replied,

"Well I could be better, but James here has been great tonight helping me along.". *"Bollocks"* thought James as Hannah turned the conversation back towards him.

"Oh yeah?", said Karen, "Your knight in shining armour is he?"

"Hardly", replied James suddenly feeling the need to make some sort of contribution, before Hannah made him sound important.

"So what exactly is the deal with you two anyway? Did he start talking and sweep you off your feet after we all left school?" asked Karen

"No actually, we haven't spoken to each other until tonight" said Hannah

"But you seem very close" pressed Karen

"I suppose we are. Just not like that. It's a little complicated and I don't want to go into it again this evening"

"Again?!" replied Karen

James responded "Yes, we've already had to explain our friendship to Hannah's fiancee tonight"

"Oh, but you said you hadn't spoken to each other ever" quizzed Karen

"We didn't say ever... look I really didn't want to go through this again today. We were friends when we were little, before we started at secondary school, that's all"

"You wouldn't even give him the time of day when I was at school, what happened?"

"Claire happened" was all that Hannah replied

"Oh..." suddenly Karen understood.

"Anyway, like I said, I don't really want to discuss it, it has been far too popular a topic of discussion this evening"

With that Karen and Hannah went to the bar, leaving James to ponder just what was going on. His old best friend and his teenage crush talking to each other at the bar chatting away, meanwhile he was stood here looking like a lost sheep. Thankfully at that moment a sound from behind him broke his concentration.

The Reunion Of A Lifetime

"Jaaaaaaaaaaaaaaaaaaaaayyyyyymmmmmmeeeessss!!!!!!" came a voice from behind him

"What?! Who is it?" said James as he spun around and saw what could only be described as a mass of hair with a voice.

"Its Rob..." spoke the hair "...Rob Headlingly! You must remember me!" and with that the mass of hair put its arm around James' shoulder.

"Rob?" said James. James had been looking at a picture of them only a hour or so ago, and yet he did not recognise the person in front of him, although that was mainly to do with the huge amount of hair obscuring his view. Rob flicked his head back and the mass of hair suddenly swung up and over his head, and finally James could see a face.

"Sorry, thought the cousin it thing would be an ice-breaker" said Rob

"Err, yeah, really good" was all that James could muster, then he thought he'd better ask "How are you doing"

"Yeah not too bad, you know, overworked and underpaid" said Rob

"What are you doing these days?"

"A bit of this and that, you know whatever comes up."

"You mean you have no career?"

"Nah, couldn't be bothered with college and a bit of bar work here and there, a few quid for helping someone move house, or cutting their lawn or whatever, it all adds up"

"Can you afford anything on that sort of money?"

"Well you know, cash in hand stuff" and he taps his nose "plus I'm technically always looking for work, so I get Jobseekers too"

"So you're scamming the system?"

"Not scamming, just playing along the thin edge of the rules"

"Sounds dodgy as heck to me"

"Yeah, well from what I hear, your money fell into your lap"

"Now wait a minute!" snapped James "I worked hard for that. It wasn't just gifted to me, I had worked my way up in the company properly. OK, so the apprentice job was given to me,

but I did everything else myself. I learnt everything about that business, I was in charge of engineering before my uncle passed away."
"No need to get defensive, I was just saying you got given most of your money"
"And I'm just saying, I got there through hard work and determination"
"Fair enough, look sorry if I sounded brash, but I can't believe you ended up a millionaire. Meanwhile I get by week to week doing odd jobs and selling duty free fags to people in the pub"
"Its not all great times and parties you know?"
"Why not? You can have whatever you want."
"You never know who to trust, who just wants to know you for your money"
"I see", said Rob. He thought for a few seconds and then said, "James?"
"What Rob?"
"Could you lend us a grand or two?" asked Rob with a grin
"Sod off" said James with a smile
"See I always told everyone you were a great guy."
"Rob isn't it?" Hannah's voice spoke from behind James.
"Yeah" said Rob
"Hi Rob" said Karen, "Me and Hannah are about to hit the dancefloor, are you coming with us?"
"Me? Dance with you? I didn't think you'd ever ask me, did you request a slow song?", Said Rob
"No you and James dance with us, as a group, we want to have some fun!"

CHAPTER 7

The Dancefloor

James and Rob were led to the dancefloor by Hannah and Karen. They had fun dancing to all manner of upbeat tunes. Whenever the DJ would slow it down, they would nip to the bar or loo and give the lovers smooching time on the dancefloor.

The evening continued with plenty of laughing and a lot of drinking. Before they knew it, it was ten to midnight and the four friends were again leaving the dancefloor as the DJ announced the final soppy song of the night. As the walked towards the bar, James turned to Hannah.

"Hannah, will you dance with me?", *Where had that come from?*
"Haven't we been dancing for a couple of hours?" said Hannah
"Yeah, but I mean this dance"
"OK...but no funny business sir"
"I would never"

And with that Hannah and James made their way back to the dancefloor as Karen and Rob stood looking on confused. James pulled Hannah close as they swayed to the song. James started talking into Hannah's ear as he held her.

"Hannah, I just wanted to say, I've had a wonderful evening and you are the best friend I could ever ask for"
"James, I'm sorry I ever lost touch with you"
"You know the real problem, don't you?"
"No, what is the real problem"
"In about ten minutes, this evening will be over, the room will

empty and people will go their separate ways"
"We won't, will we?"
"No, but reality is going to happen sooner or later and you'll have to deal with the fallout of tonight"
"Oh, yeah, I know"
"Any idea what you're going to do?"
"Not yet, obviously me and Paul are on pretty shaky ground, if there is any left there at all. But I need to deal with Claire too"
"Any idea on how to deal with Claire?"
"Machine gun?!", Hannah smiled

With that James led Hannah back to Karen and Rob who were standing at the edge of the dancefloor.

"You guys looked pretty close" said Karen
"Just needed some time to talk really" said James
"Well whatever it is, its got Hannah smiling" said Rob

Just then a big party song came on the speakers
"This is it final song of the night. Let's see you all out on the floor!" shouted the DJ over the microphone.
"Let's get back out there!" said Karen and with that the group headed back for one final song.

The final song was loud, everyone was on the dancefloor shouting and jumping around. Everyone apart from Paul and Claire who were both stood in the shadows by the door watching.

"Just friends my arse" said Paul "Did you see them?"
"Hmmm…" said Claire
"What happens now?" asked Paul
"Revenge" said Claire
"What? Here? Now?" replied paul
"No…let them have their time, I'm an expert at this."

Paul and Claire both walk back out the door and head off their separate ways.

The song finished and the DJ announced the end of the night, reminding people to not forget their coats and bags.

"So that was that" said Hannah
"It was definitely something" said James
"You are going to keep in touch Hannah, aren't you?" said Karen
"Of course, I have your number in my phone" said Hannah
"It really has been great to see you Karen" said James
"I've enjoyed it, we'll have to meet up again sometime." said Karen
"Am I going to be invited?" asked Rob
"No, I didn't enjoy spending time with you." said Karen with a grin "You prat, of course you'll be invited, I'll keep in touch with Hannah and she can keep you guys posted."

Rob turned and ran to the DJ who was starting to pack up, and came back with a scrap of paper and a pen. He starts scrawling on the paper and hands it to James.

"Here's my phone number and my email address. Let me know when you're planning a get together and I'll see if I can make it."

James opens the paper and reads it, there is a phone number at the top and then

RobTheManWithAPlan@squirrelmail.com

"That's ironic" thought James, *"Rob is the last person who'd ever have a plan"*.
"Thanks" said James
"Gotta shoot, gonna go now, I'm hoping that a mate of mine will have his cab outside and I don't want anyone else getting in it" said Rob and with that he turned and sprinted for the door.
"Well that was a sharp exit" said Karen, "anyway I should get going, you guys look after yourselves and Hannah, I'll be in touch".

Now there was just James and Hannah in the middle of an empty dancefloor. The DJ packing away, the bar staff collecting up glasses and the masses heading towards the door.

"That was a good night" said Hannah
"It was, wasn't it? Any idea what you're going to do now?"
"Not really, don't want to think about it at the moment"
"Are you going home?"
"What to a house where he might be...I hadn't really thought about it"
"You could stay at mine for tonight"
"What on the sofa"
"No, I wouldn't dream of it"
"You'd have the sofa"
"No, I can't sleep on a sofa"
"You're not suggesting I share a bed with you? I know I've had a few drinks and am a bit emotional, but that doesn't make me an easy target"
"Not at all. I have a room that is always ready for guests. Just in case we ever have unexpected business that overruns. You are welcome to stay in there, it is virtually a self contained apartment. It has king-size bed, satellite TV, en-suite, kitchenette, walk in wardrobe.."
"..OK sold, I'll come and stay at yours the night"
"Great"

James got out his phone and rang a number, he said just two words "I'm ready", and he led Hannah to the door.
"Do you have a coat to collect?" James said
"Yeah", replied Hannah "look at the queue, this could take a while"
"Nonsense, you don't have to wait when you paid for it"
"What do you mean?"
"What is your ticket number? Give it here"
Hannah handed over her ticket, James threw himself towards the counter with the ticket.
"Just need to pick this up, don't mind me"
The woman behind the counter looks up and was about to argue about cutting in when she saw who it was

"Mr. James, certainly..." she took the ticket and returned seconds later with Hannah's coat.

"Thank you very much" said James and he turned to the queue "Sorry for pushing in, Got a car waiting for me, Don't want it to get a ticket"

With that James and Hannah walked out the door and down to James' waiting driver who opened the door and they entered the car.

CHAPTER 8

The Morning After

The phone next to the bed rang loudly. Hannah looked around, not really knowing where she was, at least she'd managed to avoid a hangover. She reached over and answered the phone.

"Hello?"
"Hi, how are you doing?" came James' voice from down the phone.
"Erm, confused"
"You're in the spare room, don't you remember?"
"Oh…yeah, thanks James" Hannah said groggily.
"I'll be in the living room when you are ready to get up and about."
"OK, I suppose I need to head back at some point"
"Quite"
"I'll be down in a bit"

After a few minutes thinking about the previous evening Hannah sat up properly and looked at herself in the mirrored wardrobe door. For someone that had slept the night in her clothes on an unfamiliar bed, she didn't look too bad. Okay, her hair was a mess, her dress was clearly creased where she had laid on it and her makeup was looking tired, but all in all, she looked quite presentable. A quick tidy up with emergency makeup from her little bag, and a quick brush of the hair, a spruce up with some perfume and she was feeling much more like a human.

She headed off into the living room, James was sat on the sofa watching TV.

"What do you think? this is my second house, I bought it to have somewhere to stay near mum's, it seemed ideal last night."
"It's nice, very understated."
"You think?"
"Not really, hey what time is it anyway?"
"Quarter past twelve"
"What? Bloody hell, I'm going to have to get on"
"Any idea what you are going to do?"
"Not really, I'm still wondering about Paul"
"Aren't you engaged though?"
"Yeah, but I'm not sure if that's really on the table anymore after his behaviour last night"
"And what about Claire?"
"That bitch can go to hell for all I care, I wouldn't worry if I never saw her again"
"Fair enough...so do you want me to come with you?"
"No, best not, I don't want Paul getting any more heated than he already is."
"OK, well you know where I am if you need me."
"Err. OK, just one more question"
"What?"
"I don't know where you are if I need to. Where am I? I mean I know its your place, but I have no idea where I am. How can I even call a cab?"
"Don't worry, I will get a driver to take you back to yours." James picks up a business card from the desk in the living room and scribbles an address and his mobile on the back of it. "Are you ready to head back yet?"
"Yes, I'd better get this over with"
"OK, I'll call my driver, just head down to the door and he'll take you wherever"
"James?"
"Yes?"
"Thanks...no really, thanks. You are such a great friend, even

after all this time"
"What can I say, I have a soft spot for you" said James, with a wink. James stands up and walks over to Hannah
"Bye then" said Hannah
"Bye, and take care, and call me if you need me" said James, and with that he leans down and kisses Hannah on the forehead. Hannah shocked for a moment paused. "Sorry", said James ,"it just seemed like the right thing to do"
"No, it was nice, I really had better go"
"OK, I'll make the call"

Hannah walked to the front door and James picked up the phone and within thirty seconds there was a car waiting at the door. Hannah gave James a final wave from the door as she exited and got into the car.

CHAPTER 9

Returning Home

Hannah stepped out of the large black car onto the familiar pavement outside her house. She'd never felt this nervous about opening her own front door, not even when she'd first got the place. It seemed like it took her forever to get her key out, and turn it in the lock.

She stepped into the hallway and closed the door. The clock on the wall told her that it was nearly 3 o'clock. On any other Sunday afternoon Paul would be sat on the sofa waiting for his beloved football to be on the sports channel on the TV. Hannah didn't care for most sports, but had relented when Paul started hanging around the house a lot and had purchased a satellite package with sports to keep him happy. She peered into the living room, Paul wasn't there, not that she really expected him to be after last night. *"He has probably headed back to his parents."*, she told herself,. *"At least I don't have to deal with the fallout just yet."*

Remembering that she was still wearing last night's clothes and decided to go and take a shower. She walked up the stairs and as she got to the top of the stairs could hear the shower already on and muffled singing coming from the en-suite in the master bedroom. Paul was in the shower, *"OK, so I do have to deal with this now"* thought Hannah.

She walked into the bedroom, bed still a mess from where Paul had just got up. A faint hint of her perfume hit her, still lingering in the air from last night. She looked around the floor, a discarded suit and tie lying on the floor next to Paul's side of the bed. She sat down on the edge of the bed wondering what the next move should be. Just then the shower turned off and Paul stepped out of the shower onto the tiled floor. She saw him through the open door with his back to her grabbing a towel and starting to dry himself.

"He's quite sexy" her mind wondered "He really does have a gorgeous body. Stop It! He's an arsehole and he needs to apologise for last night"

Paul had finished drying himself and turned to face the bedroom. He looked up and saw Hannah sat on the bed.

"Have you finished having your nostalgic teenage strop?" he asked
"What?" she replied
"Have you stopped acting like a lovesick child?" he replied
"How dare you? Me acting like a child? Me?" Hannah was getting riled, this wasn't how it was supposed to work, she was going to stay calm and rational.
"Yes, you, you and your schoolgirl crush"
"Fuck you"
"No thanks" he said with a small grin
"That's not funny. You have no idea about anything do you?"
"I saw you hanging on that prick's every word last night"
"No, you saw me hanging out with my friends. My real friends, not that sham of a friend that you somehow got to hanging around with"
"Ah yes, Claire, I hadn't seen her for years. Do you know what though? Despite everything that we went through, she was supportive last night. Maybe there is something to be said for your first true love."
"To be honest, I couldn't care less about Claire, she can go to hell for all I care"
"So you don't want me inviting her over for dinner then?" Paul's

The Reunion Of A Lifetime

attempt at humour with a cheeky grin
"No, you complete idiot. I don't ever want to see that bitch again, not in the street, not at a reunion and certainly not at my house."
Paul carried on grinning and turned back towards the en-suite.
"Can we carry this on in a minute, I need the loo" he said and without waiting for an answer he closed and locked the door.

Paul's toilet breaks were stuff of legend, never less than 20 minutes, he even has some books in the bathroom in-case he gets bored.

Hannah stands up, a decision made in her mind. Paul isn't worth it, he doesn't respect her, he doesn't trust her and he is happy to hang around with people who he knows made her life hell. She starts opening the drawers and waredrobe doors, finding all of Paul's clothes that she can, she methodically removes each and every one of them and puts them in a few storage bags that she keeps under the bed.

"What is going on out there?" Paul calls from inside the bathroom
"Just sorting out some rubbish" Hannah responds

On she goes, every shirt, t-shirt, pair of trousers, shorts, boxers, socks all go into these bags. Then she goes to the laundry basket and extracts everything of Pauls, all in the same bag. Out of the bedroom she takes the bag and opens the door to the attic. Up she goes carefully, trying not to give away that she is on the stairs going up. In the attic there is an old wardrobe laying on its back, it was there when she moved in. It is just big enough to open the doors, put the bags of clothes in it and close them. It has little lock on the door, so she locks the door and pockets the key and sneaks back down the stairs. A quick double check ensures that she hasn't missed anything. There are no clothes of Paul's left in easy reach in the house. Then she picks up his keys from the bedside and removes her door key from the oversized bunch and takes them with her. She heads downstairs and puts the keys on the hook by the front door where they are usually left.

Ten minutes later, a voice calls down the stairs "Fucking hell, where are they?"
"What?" Hannah replies
"My clothes, where are they?"

Hannah walks out of the kitchen into the hall where Paul is now standing at the bottom of the stairs completely naked.

"What have you done with my clothes?"
"I don't know what you mean" Hannah said with a wry grin.
"Stop playing games with me" said Paul
"OK, They are in a bag just outside the front door"
Paul looks at the door desperately
"Outside?!"
"Yes, outside"
"Enough messing around, are you going to get them for me?"
"Errr.... I think not"

Paul looks through the spy hole and can see a carrier bag in the middle of the front garden. If he covers himself with the table mat from the little table in the hall, he can make this. He grabs his keys from the hook, just in-case. He makes a dash out into the garden with a table mat held in front of him. Hannah pushes the door closed behind him and latches it too for good measure and then dives up the stairs.

"OK" Paul thinks, I'm locked out but the clothes are just there.

The bedroom window opens upstairs, Hannah is laughing at Paul. She is holding up her phone recording what happens next.

So, over to the bag he goes whilst still holding the table mat to cover his little dignity he has left, he struggles to open up the bag single handed.

"Fuck!" the bag contains nothing but a load of kitchen scraps, old tea-bags, potato peelings and orange peel mainly. So now, here he is locked out the front of the house with no clothes on.

Hannah continues filming from the upstairs window
"You know what Paul, I would say you aren't worth it, but this is hilarious"
"Fucking help me. You can't leave me like this"
"Why not, this embarrassment is a fraction of how I felt last night when you were kicking off"
"No really, help me"
"OK, I'll give you one item, my choice"

Hannah looks around, she really doesn't want to give him any clothes, and that would mean going back into the attic. Then she sees it, his precious mobile phone.

"You get one shot to catch this!" She said with glee and held up his phone
"No, don't throw it" he responds

It is too late she is already winding up her throw, right towards the far left corner of the garden. He sees it and runs, diving for it, dropping the table mat in the process, his modesty all but forgotten. He just manages to catch the phone.

"You bitch!" he shouts holding his phone and curling himself up like a ball on the floor to try and remain at least slightly decent.

"Call your brother or your Dad, get them to take you home!"

Paul presses the screen on his phone to make a call and speaks
"She's thrown me out, can you get round here?"
Hannah can't hear the response
"No, no, nothing like that, just get round here quick and hit the horn when you are outside and I'll jump in. I'll explain when you get here"

"Obviously, the engagement's off" said Hannah out the window

Paul crouches behind the bush at the front of the garden clutching his phone and keys. He turns and says, "What about my wallet?"

"Hang on"

Hannah gets the wallet off of the bedside, removes her credit cards from it and the cash that was in it. After all, she'd taken that money out last night for them to use at the reunion. She goes back to the window and calls out

"Paul, here's your wallet" and throws it with expert precision into the right hand corner of the garden completely opposite to where Paul is hiding and it lands in the bird bath.

"Oh great, thanks" says Paul sarcastically. "I'll get that in a minute"

Just then a sports car pulls up outside and a beep of the horn blares out.

"That's none of his family's cars" thought Hannah.

Paul dives through the gate and into the passenger seat.

"Shit! my wallet, it's in the bird bath", he says as he closes the door

The drivers door opens and out steps Claire. She walks around the car along the path and reaches over the hedge and grabs the sopping wet wallet out of the bird bath. She looks up at Hannah who is still filming everything and smirks at the camera. She turns, gets back in the car and drives off.

Hannah stops recording, she feels victorious but empty. The battle has taken it out of her and seeing Claire has taken the wind completely out of her sails.

CHAPTER 10

Call On A Friend

Hannah sits on the side of the bed looking at the business card in her hand. She turns it over and enters the number into her phone memory.

She decides she really needs a shower. "A clean body, for a clean start" she tells herself. She walks into the bathroom and sees the wet towel left on the floor by Paul. She picks it up takes it into the bedroom and throws it into the hamper. She should feel sad about it but she doesn't she feels like she is taking control. She walks back into the bathroom, gets undressed and climbs in to the shower.

When she emerges, she feels far better for getting clean. She dries herself and wanders back into her bedroom. She gets her phone off of the bedside and sends James a message

"Hi, its Hannah"

A few seconds later the response comes

"How are you"
"Fine, Paul is gone"
"Gone? Was he already gone when you got there?"
"No, but I reckon he wishes he was"
"Really? What did you do?"

She finds the video on her phone and hits the share button. She can't help watching it back again.

"Fuck me, that's hilarious" comes the response
"Did you watch to the end?"
"Only until the car pulls up"
"Keep watching"

There is pause whilst James watches it and processes what is on the screen"

"Fucking hell, he called Claire!"

It is then that Hannah notices it. On her dresser, he favourite perfume is missing. She knows it was there last night, she used it and then left it there and took her little emergency bottle with her in her bag.

"Where would her perfume have gone?" she thought. Then it started to dawn on her, "...That fucking bitch!...and that little weasel!"

"Fucking hell!" Hannah writes "Claire spent the night here with him"
"What? Did he tell you?"
"No, I'm not certain, but pretty much"
"Someone had been using my perfume this morning and it is gone, and watch the video again, listen to the phone call he makes, no details or address and Claire knows exactly where I live?"
"Oh, wow. I see what you mean"
"So what can we do about it?"
"We can't do this over a text conversation on a phone. Pub?"
"OK"
"I'll be there soon"
"How do you know where I live?"
"I don't, but my driver does :-D, I'll be there soon"

A while later James' car pulls up outside and out he gets, he leans into the window and speaks to the driver and off the car goes. He walks up the path to the front door and rings the bell.

Hannah opens the door and grins at her friend. She is stood there in Jeans and a t-shirt.

"Looking good for a pub lunch" says James
"Even if it is a little late for lunch" says Hannah
"Well, have you eaten yet?"
"No, couldn't stomach it earlier, but am starting to get hungry now"
"That's settled then, where's your local?"
"I thought you'd know somewhere"
"No, I'm supplying the finances and the friendship, you need to suggest the venue"
"We'll go to the old mill, it is only a short walk along the river at the bottom of the road and it really is lovely in there, if a little pricey, but if you're paying" Hannah grins
"Why not?" James smiles back and they turn and walk back out of the door.

They walked together down the road and along the river. Hannah spent the entire time describing how Paul had gone to the loo and she'd hidden all of his clothes.

"Are you going to give them back?" asks James
"Maybe, eventually" says Hannah
"Remind me not to get on the wrong side of you." says James
"Why not?"
"Because you have a sadistic streak"
"Yeah, I suppose, but he deserved it and was so much fun to watch!"

The walk into the bar and find themselves a quiet corner. James asks Hannah what she wants and heads off to the bar. He comes back with drinks in hand and resumes the conversation.

"So what now?" he asks
"Getting on with my new life" she responds
"No regrets about today?"

"None at all"
"Are you really sure you want to close the door on Paul?"
"He doesn't trust me, he has hidden stuff from me and he seems to have found a friend in Claire, if not more than a friend"
"OK, so that's a no to Paul then"
"No to Paul"
"So why are you still wearing the ring?"

Hannah hadn't even noticed, she'd been wearing the ring for so long, it was just an extension of her person. She'd not considered that it was actually part of her relationship with Paul

"Bloody hell, good point" and with a little difficulty she removed the ring and put it in her purse.
"How long had you been engaged?" asked James
"A little over three years"
"Had you made wedding plans?"
"Not really, I was going to get people's contact details last night so I could get in touch when we'd set the date"
"So you did intend to get married?"
"Well we got engaged ages ago as we thought I may be pregnant and Paul wanted to do the honorable thing, but once it was clear I wasn't, I don't think he was interested any longer."
"So what life just went on?"
"Yeah, he'd moved in and so we were living together in my house"
"How was living together?"
"Well, we both worked then we got in, one of us would make dinner, we might hang around together and watch TV but by the end most of the time Paul would just go out with his mates"
"Sounds like you were just in a cosy place"
"A cosy place?"
"Yeah, you spend so long with someone, you get into the routine and act being in a relationship even though you are just going through the motions"
"Maybe...So tell me, how does someone like you get so wise

about these things?"
"Someone like me?"
"You know, single, unattached"
"I don't know, observation mainly"
"What do you mean?"
"OK, watch this"

James points across the room

"The man at the end of the bar is either recently separated from his wife or is sneaking around"
"Wedding ring mark on the finger?"
"Exactly, but more than that, smart white shirt, suggests he looks after his appearance, but nothing about his demeanor suggests that he would iron his shirts"
"Right so what are you saying"
"Either he sends his laundry out, or his wife irons his shirts and he is playing away"
"But he's by himself, isn't he?"
"At the moment...I've seen it time after time."

At that moment their food arrives.and they both get distracted by baskets of chicken and chips.

"Nothing like good pub grub" says James
"I haven't eaten out like this in ages" replies Hannah
"Neither have I" says James "it's not much fun without someone with you"

They eat their food and drink their drink and conversation turns to mundane things such as what they'd been watching on TV. It turned out they both liked the same crime dramas on TV and had been following them intently.

"I'm sure I could get advanced copies if I paid the right person at the BBC" says James
"You could do that?"
"Probably, but I enjoy the cliffhangers and the anticipation,

once you box set it, that's all gone"
"I suppose"

A young woman in a short skirt wanders into the bar and walks up to the married man. The man leans over and kisses her and orders a drink for her from the bartender. James raises his eyebrows at Hannah. She giggles and the couple look around to see what is going on. Both of them look away quickly.

"So what do you think….Daughter?" says Hannah
"Hardly", says James, "did you not notice the hand?"
"What hand?"
"He squeezed her arse as he kissed her"
"He did not!" exclaims Hannah "she's half his age"
"And the rest" says James
"So do you think she's in it for money?"
"Possibly, or what he can buy her, or maybe he makes her feel good about herself. It could be love of course, but who knows? He certainly hasn't made a commitment to her, if he is still with his wife"
"Maybe I'll ask her" says Hannah
"Maybe we can play detectives"
"Oooo, this is fun."

They carry on eating and drinking, keeping half an eye on the couple, and then the woman heads to the toilet.

"Here's a chance" says James
"I'm already on it" says Hannah
"Another drink when you get back" says James
"Definitely" says Hannah

Hannah gets up from the table and heads to the toilet.
She goes in the stall and waits for the toilet in the neighbouring stall to flush, she flushes hers and walks out and washes her hands. Out comes the woman and stands next to her at the sink.

"Nice place isn't it?" says Hannah

The Reunion Of A Lifetime

"Yeah, I really like it. Nick always meets me here" says the woman

"Nick, is that the guy you're with at the bar?"

"Yeah, every two weeks we come here for an evening then off to his hotel room. He spends all his time away on business. He doesn't even have a house! I have to catch him when he's here"

"Sorry, must introduce myself properly, I'm Shelly" says Hannah

"Caitlin" replies the girl "I've never seen you here before"

"No, this is my first time here in ages"

"Hope you enjoy it. Oh, if you are going for a desert, their death by chocolate looks delicious"

"Not today, but I'll keep it in mind, thanks"

The two of them leave the toilet and head back to their respective tables.

Meanwhile James had been to the bar.
"Two rum and cokes please" he says to the bartender

He turns around to the fellow at the bar, "Do you want a drink fella?"

"What?"

"Sorry, do you and your friend want a drink? I feel like maybe myself and my friend interrupted you earlier with our laughing and I wanted to apologise"

"Oh, that's very kind, no harm done, I really didn't think much of it"

"I'm Peter" said James

"Steve" said the guy at the bar "I haven't seen you around here before"

"No, I just met up with an old friend. You come here often?"

"When I'm away on business I come here and stay in the hotel down the road"

"Well nice to meet you anyway, what do you want?"

"I'll have a pint and Caitlin will have a gin and tonic, thank you."

The bartender started pouring their drinks.

"Enjoy" said James ", and sorry again about earlier"
"No problem" says Steve

James walks back to the table just as Hannah and Caitlin walk back in.

"So what do we know?" asks James
"Her name is Caitlin" says Hannah
"Confirmed"
"He is Nick"
"No, he said his name was Steve"
"No!" says Hannah "Did you find if he has a wife?"
"Not really, but I think he does" says James "He comes here whilst away on business"
"Caitlin said he meets her here most weeks but he said to her that he is always away on business and never goes home"
"Sounds like he's on the fiddle somewhere, different names, different stories. Should we push it any further?"
"No, it sounds like they meet here, maybe we should be here next time"
"Ooooo, I like your style"

James gets out his phone.

"What are you doing" asks Hannah
"Making notes"

James taps away at his phone. Caitlin, knows him as Nick, introduced himself as Steve. Must remember my name is Peter.

"Did you use your real name?" asks James
"No, I'm Shelly" replies Hannah

James adds to his notes. Hannah is Shelly. James presses save and then looks up.

"This is fun, real life mystery solving." says James

"You could do anything with your money" says Hannah

"But this, this is real life"

"And someone could be getting hurt" says Hannah suddenly thinking of the man's wife.

"And it is our duty to ensure that the truth comes out"

"Quite"

"So is this a regular thing now?"

"Seems like it"

"Good, I'm enjoying it," says James. He looks at the empty baskets and glasses "So what now?"

"Let's get out of here and go back to mine" says Hannah "I need to do something, but I don't want to be there alone just yet."

"OK"

As they leave they wave bye to their new friends, deliberately avoiding using names. They wander back along the river and up the road back to Hannah's house.

CHAPTER 11

Clearing Out

When they get back to the house, Hannah pauses on the doorstep. She takes a deep breath and unlocks the door.

"OK, we're in, now what" says James
"Bedroom" says Hannah
"What?" says James
"I need your help in the bedroom"
"OK...I'm flattered, but a rebound isn't what you need"
"No, stupid... I need you to help me with something"
"I knew that" says James with a grin
"Yeah, right, you're a bloke, you were thinking with your dick" says Hannah
"Maybe a little" admits James
"Look, we're friends, nothing else"
"Apart from mystery detectives"
"Well that too, I suppose" says Hannah with a smile

Hannah leads James up to the bedroom and opens a hamper at the end of the bed and takes out sheets and pillow cases.

"I need to get this bedding off of my bed, especially now I know she's been here." says Hannah
"OK, why does this need me?" asks James
"A king size bed is normally a two person job, especially where I'm concerned" says Hannah
"What do you mean?"
"If I do it, everytime I put one corner on, another shoots off. It is

like a bad clown act"
"Fair enough, I'll help then"

Between them it still takes some time to get everything changed, the duvet was seemingly impossible to find the corners in and somehow at one point James ended up inside the duvet cover, but they got there eventually.

"OK" says James "what are we going to do with the old stuff?"
"Burn it" says Hannah
"It seems like a waste"
"I suppose, but I don't want it anymore. It will always remind me of what has happened"
"OK, let's get it washed and give it to charity then"
"I hadn't thought of that, I really don't want it around any longer though, I certainly don't have any intention of washing it here"
"That's ok, I'll get someone to collect it and they can deal with it"
"Do you just have people for everything?"
"No not really, but driving, laundry, cleaning, yeah"
"So do you do anything yourself?"
"Of course! I can get myself dressed, work and I cook my own food normally...and I even wash up too"
"I thought you'd just have a cook to deal with lunch"
"Never, I love cooking, it's very theraputic"
"Are you going to invite me over for a meal sometime then?"
"Has anyone ever told you that you are very pushy?"
"Yeah, you, when we were about eight years old" says Hannah with a big smile. James grins back.
"Anyone else?"
"Not that I can remember" she replies. James smiles, turns, picks up a pillow and hits her around the head with it.
"I've missed this" says James
"Me too" says Hannah

Hannah looks at the clock. "Shit! Its half past nine, where did the

afternoon and evening go?"
"I don't know, but I've had fun"
"Me too"
"I suppose I'd better get back to mine"
"I suppose so, I've got work in the morning, I should go to bed"
"Will you be ok?"
"Of course, I have been on my own before you know"
"Well, let me know if there is anything I can do to help"

James pulled out his phone and pressed a button on the screen.

"What's that?" asks Hannah
"Speed recall for my driver"
"So what, he waits around all day for you to call?"
"No, I told him to go home and I'd let him know if I need him to pick me up, he gets paid even when he is at home, as I don't think its fair for him to be asked to drop everything at a moment's notice. He can always say he's busy and I'll call another driver instead"
"If...."
"What?"
"You said, if, if I need him to pick me up. Was there a chance that you wouldn't need to be picked up?"
"I didn't know, I thought maybe you'd be glad of the company and I'd sleep on the sofa"

James' phone beeps.

"He'll be here in 5 minutes" says James.
"Are you going to take this bedding then?" asks Hannah
"OK, get a bag or something to put it in"
"Great", Hannah digs around under the bed and retrieves a bag. She begins stuffing all the bedding into it, "Do you want the clothes too?" she asks, suddenly remembering them in the attic.
"No, best not, after all you might want to hold them to ransom"
"Good point"
"I'll tell you what I have noticed"

"What?"
"No attempt to call you, at all. He knows he's in the wrong"
"Hmmmm", says Hannah, "I hadn't really considered that. Thanks again for today"

Just then James' phone beeps

"My car is outside"
They walk down the stairs
"Thanks again for today"
"You already said that"
"I know, but I just want you to know that I really appreciate it"
"If you need help, call me"
"OK, its a deal"

Hannah opens the door and wanders down the path with his carrier bag in hand and gets into the waiting car. He waves as the door closes. Hannah waves back, and then his car pulls away.

Hannah closes the door and turns back into the house. She is exhausted, lonely, but generally happy. She heads off to bed feeling positive and looking forward to what tomorrow will bring.

CHAPTER 12

Monday Morning

The loud ringing of the doorbell wakes Hannah from her sleep. She looks across at her phone on the bedside, 6:45am, *"Who is ringing my doorbell at this time of the morning?"*. Then the knocking begins too alternate ringing of the doorbell and knocking on the door.

Hannah throws on her nightie and looks out of the window. There by the front door is Paul in a pair of old jeans and a t-shirt. Hannah opens the window

"What are you doing here?", she shouts down
"Where's my key?"
"My key. It's my house therefore my key, you are no longer living here, so no key"
"Let me in"
"Why would I want to do that?"
"I need some clothes, I've got nothing for work"
"Small problem there, I've looked through all of the drawers and the wardrobe as you did yesterday and there just doesn't seem to be any of your clothes anywhere"
"Stop pissing around and just give me the clothes back"
"I told you, they aren't there"
"What did you do with them?"
"Now if only I could remember. Oh actually, I've got a similar question, what happened to my perfume?"
"Your perfume? How the fuck would I know?"
"It was there on Saturday evening, it wasn't there when I got

back yesterday"

"So, you probably put it somewhere else"

"Ah, but also there was a distinct smell of it having been used yesterday in the bedroom when I came in"

"I still have no idea what you are talking about"

"Fine, thanks for your assistance, I'm going back in now"

"No, I need my clothes…" Paul's voice tailed off as Hannah closed the window. She turned picked up her phone and wandered into the bathroom.

"Oh well, the alarm was going to go off any second anyway"

She turned the phone alarm off and sat down on the toilet looking around the bathroom. Paul's shaving gel and razor, his shower gel, his shampoo they were all still in their places. Not that it really bothered her, but they were still there, like he was still part of the household. She grabbed everything that she could identify as his and put them in the bin.

"Great a clean start, for a new day" she thought.

She got herself showered, dressed, went downstairs, got her coffee and her breakfast and put the radio on. Some cheery voice introducing middle of the road songs on what they promise to be a bright morning. Hannah was immune to the inane banter on the radio as she finished off her make-up. She was deep in thought, not thinking of Paul or James or even Claire, but of Caitlin and the mystery man.

She wondered was there somebody getting hurt in all this. Whether the man does have a wife, or different girls in every town. Maybe in all of this Caitlin was the victim and doesn't know she's the bit on the side, or maybe she's the relationship being cheated on. This was so complicated, she must ask James next time she speaks to him, what his opinion is.

Anyway, a glance at the clock told her, she really should head for the office. She got up, gave herself a check over in the mirror, *"I really do look great for 41"*, she thought to herself. She walked over to the front door opened the lock and stepped out, closing the door behind her.

She looked around, no sign of Paul, *"well at least he didn't hang around"* she thought as she walked to her car and got in. She drove off down the road starting her day with determination.

Since leaving the previous evening James had felt really positive about everything. He was back in contact with people he hadn't seen in years and had helped Hannah in her time of need. However, this morning he was feeling empty. He had no need to head back up the country today, he'd carried out the early morning manufacturing meetings by video call over the internet and they had passed without incident. A few bits here and there but nothing he couldn't leave his team with.

He was now sat behind his desk looking at his laptop, reading his schedule for the day....bugger all. If he was at the office he'd go for a walk through engineering, talk to some of the guys up in technical and see if he could help anyone. But he wasn't at the office, he was at his second home. With nothing else planned, he sent an email to his secretary saying he had been delayed and wouldn't be back for a few days but would keep an eye on everything. Having cleared himself of any responsibility for a few days, he started playing around on the computer, visiting social networking sites, adding as many people as he could from the reunion. It was about twenty minutes later a notification popped up that Hannah had accepted his request. Suddenly he felt a warm fuzzy feeling. He clicked on her name and started trawling through the posts online.

Her list was mainly inspirational quotes and poster images, there were occasional pictures of her and Paul from Christmas and Birthdays and the like, then a few pictures of her and her mum together on Hannah's 21st birthday. Suddenly a rush of emotion as he remembered hanging around with Hannah and her mum as kids. Her mum was so cool, she had vimto, no one else ever let him drink vimto. His mum only ever had cheap supermarket own brand blackcurrant if he was lucky, it was normally cheap orange squash or water at home. He had become so caught up in the feelings of nostalgia and his mind was whisked away thinking of being 8 and 9 and playing in gardens, having fun, silly dances. After a bit he came back to reality and carried on scrolling down the page and then there it was, a picture of Hannah at no more than 7 or 8 years old playing on his swing in his garden. He wasn't tagged the picture, but it was unmistakably his house. He remembered that picture being taken, and he realised why he wasn't in the image. He was hiding behind a bush in the corner, waiting to leap out as the swing went backwards. Just after the picture was taken, he'd jumped out and Hannah nearly came off the swing, the panic and cascades of tears from her had got him in so much trouble that day. What else could he do? He clicked on the bush in the picture and tagged himself.

Hannah was at work, she knew she shouldn't be on her phone but she was paranoid that Paul would try and call her so was checking her phone every thirty seconds, but then the notification had appeared that James wanted to link with her. She clicked yes and didn't think anything of it. A short while later another notification, "James has liked a picture of you". She clicked it, her 21st, she really missed her mum, it was times like these when she could go and see her mum and have a cup of tea and talk about things. She suddenly felt the need to be alone, she dashed off to the toilet and locked herself in the cubicle. Her phone vibrated again, another notification, "James has tagged himself in a picture of yours". *"That's odd, James isn't in any of my pictures"* she thought to herself. She tapped the screen and up appeared the picture of the swing. She sat there staring at the picture. *"James isn't in this picture"* she thought to herself. She scanned the picture but couldn't see him anywhere. She was aware that it was James' mum's garden, maybe he'd made a mistake and was trying to set the location. She clicked the menu at the top of the screen, show tags. Her name appeared above her head, and James' name appeared above a bush at the side of the picture. *"Oh my god"* suddenly tears were pouring down her cheeks as the emotion of being scared on the swing filled her. She had totally forgotten that day, yet in a moment that image had taken on a very different feeling.

"I must get a grip" she thought, she sat there and eventually slowly regained her composure. It took her around 5 minutes to calm herself down, she dried her eyes and stared at the phone. Another notification, "You and James are both tagged in a new picture", she clicked the button. A picture appeared of James stood on stage at the reunion, Hannah holding his hand tightly. Underneath the picture was the description "How did a geek like him end up with her?". Under that, she could see people commenting.

"Did you see what happened?"
"When she smacked Claire? That was awesome!"
"No, much earlier, I don't think many people were there. It turns out Hannah was engaged to some other bloke and had been sleeping with James the whole time. There was a huge fight and the other guy stormed out"
"Was he the bloke that followed Claire later?"
"Don't know, that sounds like some sort of crazy orgy setup if you ask me"

Hannah couldn't take this, everyone had the wrong end of the stick, she had to respond. But before she got a chance to the next comment was from James.

"Hannah and me are friends, have been since we were babies. Most of you didn't know at school as we drifted apart for a while, quite a while. Saturday was the first time we'd seen each other since school. I know you guys will make a story out of anything, but really there is nothing to it. We are friends. Oh and if anyone tries to defend Claire or Paul, Hannah will slap them! :-D"

Hannah smiled, tapped the comment button and just put "Well said James!". She stood up feeling far better about herself, she had decided to stop worrying about Paul. She washed her hands, put her phone on silent and went back about her work for the afternoon.

James had been adding Rob, Karen and anyone he could find to his various social networks, obviously this was a great use of time as a director of a busy company. He'd been accepted by many people as they'd seen it, then someone started tagging him. Pictures from the reunion, mostly him dancing, a few of him at the bar and then one of him on stage with Hannah holding his hand. When he saw the comments, he knew he had to stop them now. He didn't want Hannah seeing them, especially with everything that had happened yesterday. Once he'd posted his comment, he felt quite pleased with himself. Then Hannah's reply appeared and he felt warm and fuzzy again.

He resisted the temptation to call Hannah or even text her, he didn't want to be too full on. She had other people to support her, maybe she needs to spend time with them. He decided to send a text to Rob.

"Hi mate, James here, fancy going to the pub and catching the football tonight?"

Not that James cared much for football, unless it was an international game. He didn't follow any club, but he guessed that Rob did.

"Hi, can do, if ur buying ;-) u heard anything from anyone?"
"No, weekend was all quiet. Whereabouts are you, what's your local?"
"Meet at the Bull, d'ya know Winstone town?"
"No, but I'll meet you there, shall we say 7:30?"
"OK, dont turn up dressed smart, youll get a kicking"

So his evening was planned, a night out with Rob in a noisy pub with football on. Not exactly high on his list, but at least he's getting out.

CHAPTER 13

A Night In The Pub

James had hired a mid range car to go to the pub. He thought turning up with a private driver could give off the wrong impression. He pulled into the car park and stepped out of the car. He was wearing chinos, a polo shirt and a pair of trainers, seemed casual enough. The time was 7:25, he was five minutes early. He decided to wait in the car for a second.

He saw groups of young lads going in, dressed in football shirts. *"Why do they do that?"* though James, *"It's not like they are playing the game, why do they wear the kit?"*. He watched as Rob sauntered along the road and stepped into the bar. James stepped out of the car and locked it behind himself.

He wandered around to the front door of the bar and stepped in. It was the noise that hit him first, groups of football fans cheering in front of a giant projector screen at one end of the room. The smell was next, that slightly stale lager smell that seemed to be present in some bars. He looked up and apart from the football fans at one end of the room, the bar was actually quite nice. He got the feeling that if it wasn't for the match being on, there may only have been 2 people in the bar plus him and Rob.

Rob was leaning against the bar, chatting to the bartender. He turned and clocked James as he walked in.

"Here he is! Right on cue" says Rob
"Rob here was about to be thrown out for coming in and not buying anything" says the bartender

"Is that a normal occurance?" asks James
"He has a tab longer than than his arm" said the bartender "he promises to settle it every time he gets paid, then he goes on a bender and spends it all and adds some more on to the tab"
"What is his tab at anyway?" says James. The bartender opens a little book under the counter.
"Just over two hundred and ninety quid" says the bartender. Rob looks at James with a grin.
"Wow!", says James,"Anyway what do you want to drink?"
"Lager, please" says Rob. James turns to the bartender
"Can I have a lager and a coke please?" says James
"Certainly sir, anything else?"
"Not at the moment"

The bartender pours the drinks and James hands the pint of lager over to Rob.

"Thanks." says Rob "For a minute, I thought you were going to pay my tab"
"Get real!" says James "I don't like you that much you know." and he grins at Rob
"Hey!" replies Rob "I thought we were friends"
"I told you, I'm not being friends with you just to give you money" says James
"OK, OK, shall we find a table?"
"Come on then"

To James' surprise Rob took a seat at the quiet end of the pub at a table. James sat down opposite him.

"Not interested in the match?" asks James
"A little but not interested in the crush down that end"
"So how are you going to watch it?". Rob, points over James' shoulder to a small tv hung from the end of the bar.
"No one ever notices that TV. I always sit down this end, anyway I got the feeling you weren't here for the match. So what do you want to talk about?"

"Did you look at pictures from reunion online?"
"Nah, try to stay off it as much as I can, only ever go on there if someone asks me to, in person"
"Ahh so that's why you haven't responded to my request?"
"Probably, so what's up?"
"Look at this"

James opens the picture of him on stage with Hannah.

"They're right, I'd never have given you a chance of you ending up with her" says Rob
"No, but I'm not with her, am I?"
"Well, no, you made that quite clear"
"I'm just helping out a friend"
"That picture does look a little cosy though"
"I know, but anyway I have something else to ask you. What do you think of Karen?"
"Karen? Yeah, she's great"
"Do you think I'd have a chance with her?"
"A better question is do you even know her?"
"Well, no, but then most people don't know me either"
"I have to be honest and say I don't see you two together. I just don't think you're her type."
"Really, and what would her type be?"
"You know, bit of a drifter, a down and out looking for a mother figure to look after him, someone like…I don't know, me maybe?"
"You?!"
"Yeah, why not?"
"I just don't get it, why would anyone choose you over me?" says James "I mean obviously you're a nice guy, but so am I and I have money"
"Yeah but it isn't just about being a nice guy" says Rob "you've got to have the right attitude, be the right person, it's all about swagger and feel"
"Interesting, so you think you have something I don't?"

"I think so"

"So you think Karen would go out with you given a chance?"

"Absolutely!" Rob said this with such confidence that James wasn't sure if he was being an arsehole or just totally convinced of his ability.

"OK, I tell you what, I'll ask Hannah to talk to Karen and if she agrees to a date with you and actually turns up, I will pay your bar tab and for the evening out, regardless of how the evening turns out.", Rob is stunned at this statement is about to accept when James continues, "However if she doesn't agree or turn up, then you need to teach me what you think makes you so special, so I know what to avoid doing!" James smirks

"OK, it's a deal" says Rob "but it has to be a genuine request, I don't want you scuppering it deliberately"

"I promise, anyway I won't be doing the asking, Hannah will", and with that James pulled out his phone and started tapping away.

Hannah was sat on the sofa in the front room, looking at her phone, willing it to ring. She just wanted contact from someone. She'd been with Paul for so long, she'd forgotten what it was like to be alone. She'd heated up some soup for tea, not really liking the idea of slaving away in a kitchen over a meal just for her.

She opened up her social feed and started looking through the pictures from the reunion again. So many people, people she'd once called friends, now just friends in her online groups. There were great pictures of the night and people commenting left right and centre. The picture walls had got people started on digging out their own old high school pictures too and posting those online. She spent what felt like 5 minutes but was more like an hour trawling over the pictures and trying to ignore any of the old pictures that had her being buddies with Claire in them.

Then she got a notification, another response to the picture

The Reunion Of A Lifetime

of her and James on stage. This one was from Claire and the reply was a picture of its own, Hannah and James in a deep embrace during that final slow dance whispering into each other's ears. Underneath the caption "Whatever you say James". Hannah was shocked, that moment was so personal, she hadn't even considered that someone would take a picture of it. Her blood was boiling, Claire was so under her skin, she didn't know what to do.

Seconds later her phone went again, a text message this time from James. She wasn't sure she could face it, not on top of the pictures and Claire's little comment. She decided not to open it, instead she started flicking around the channels on the TV. She happened upon a romantic comedy that she'd seen years before. Her and Paul had gone to the cinema together to watch it. She'd loved it and absolutely fell in love with it, but she got the feeling that Paul wanted to watch the action film in the next screen. It wasn't that Paul wasn't romantic, just that he had his own ideas of what was entertaining and two hours of will they, won't they obviously wasn't his. She had the film on DVD, she'd bought it on release day, Paul said it was a waste of money "It'll be half that price if you'd waited a few weeks" was all that she could remember him saying about it. But Paul wasn't here anymore so she was watching it on TV, enjoying every moment, feeling that emotional investment in the characters like she'd never been allowed to before. When the film finished, it was getting late so she took herself off to bed floating in the feelings of a wonderful love story.

James and Rob watched the match in the pub. James even found himself getting into the game. During half time, James had asked Rob what he'd actually been up to since school.

"I told you, anything I like"
"Yeah but you can't just do that, you've got to have worked at some point"
"Well yeah, when I left school I carried on working for the news-

agents for a couple of years"
"That didn't pay well, you were part-time weren't you?"
"Then Jean retired and they needed someone to work full-time and learn to run the business for them"
"Sounds good, what happened"
"It was the newsagents near the school, I was so much cooler than Jean was. I pretended not to notice when the kids pinched the odd chocolate bar"
"Pretended not to notice?"
"Jean was such a stick, she'd have you banned for so much as looking at a bar without enough cash"
"So what happened?"
"I pretended not to notice the porn mags inside the computer games magazines"
"...and?"
"The bloody bitch had covert CCTV put in one weekend and watched me on the camera not stopping it happening"
"That's not your fault if she couldn't prove you knew"
"I got the mags down for the lad, then turned away whilst he hid them"
"Ah....so busted then?"
"Just a little, she didn't pay me my last week's wages, said I owed her at least that much in cash"
"I think you got off lightly"
"Lightly? DSS said I could claim on the dole as I'd made myself jobless"
"They have a point, what did you do next?"
I worked behind the bar here for 3 months."
"How did that work out?"
"Well, you know, I'm behind a bar, everyone else is drinking, I helped myself to a few drinks"
"So you stole them?"
"No, I had every intention of paying out of my wages, it was an arrangement we had"
"So what happened?"
"I drank more than I earned...for four weeks in a row. I ended

up owing them fifty quid instead of getting paid for any of my work. I paid it off eventually"
"Otherwise we wouldn't be here now, with your oversized bar tab"
"Which you will pay when I go on a date"
"Don't count your chickens...you've got to get a date first"

By the end of the match, Rob had managed four pints, all at James' expense. James had been drinking soft drinks all night, as he had to drive back afterwards. James walked out of the pub whilst Rob stumbled along behind him.

"Let's get a kebab" shouted Rob
"What? No" replied James
"But I really fancy one"
"I'm not surprised, you're blasted"
"Have you ever thought about that?"
"What?"
"You can take any object, make it into an action and it is another word for pissed"
"Not sure I follow"
"Take an object, add ed to the end of it and call me it"
"Hmmm," James paused and thought "You're lamp-posted"
"Yeah, completely lamp-posted, I'd go as far as to say I'm car-parked!" replied Rob
"Very good" said James

James roots around in his wallet and pulls out a tenner.

"Look Rob, its getting late, and some of us have to work tomorrow and haven't been drinking" says James "So take this money and get a kebab. I'll let you know when I hear anything back from Hannah"
"Don't try to wriggle out of our bet"
"No chance, this is fun, I want to see the maestro in action"
"See ya later mate!" yelled Rob as James turned to head for his car

"Yeah, see you soon", yelled James over his shoulder as he rounded the corner back towards the pub car park.

CHAPTER 14

Shell Shock

James woke up momentarily, flashing lights and someone telling him to stay calm, he blacked out again.

His eyes opened again momentarily, laying on his back with strip lights passing above him, then he was gone again.

The next time he opened his eyes, a nurse was stood next to the bed.

"Urrrrrrgggghhh" said James
"Don't speak, and try not to worry", said the nurse, "I'll go and get the doctor, he can explain everything"

James sat there trying to take it all in, he was in a hospital bed, hooked up to all kinds of monitors. He was in a side room, obviously been under significant observation. There was a police officer sat on the other side of the room. His head hurt, but then that could be the incessant beeping of the machines around him.

The nurse comes back in followed by a doctor.

"You see, nice and awake now" says the nurse
"I'm very pleased to see that" says the doctor "Now sir, lets start at the top, can you remember your name"
"James"
"...and your surname?"
"Richardson"
"Good, good, and the first line of your address"

"I don't give my address out unless necessary"
"Totally understandable, but you do know where you live don't you?"
"Yes, I do"
"Who is the prime minister?"
"Margaret Thatcher" says James "...just kidding" and he pulls a grin
"Hmmm" says the doctor "I'm just going to check your eyes". The doctor holds James' left eye open and shines a light into it, he then moves over and does the same with the right.
"Much better, no signs of any lasting effects" says the Doctor
"I'm guessing you have a hell of a headache though?"
"Well the machines aren't helping"
"No, well I don't think we need you attached to them any more"

The nurse nods her head to the doctor

"You sir are very lucky indeed, a touch harder or a bit to one side or the other, who knows what state you would have been in" says the Doctor "anyway, all looks fine now", he picks up the chart and scribbles something on it. "Ok Mr Richardson, I'm sure the officer wants to speak to you, but just take your time and when you are ready, the nurse here can get someone to come and collect you, they'll need to stay with you for 24 hours mind."

The doctor turned and headed for the door, the nurse started disconnecting the machines. She unplugged the a heart monitor lead from James' chest and the machine let out a high pitched alarm

"Shit!", says the nurse, and hits the power switch on the unit, "turn the machine off before disconnecting the leads. Sorry, I imagine that went right through you."

The nurse continues unplugging the equipment and then says "I'd say you are lucky to have got away with a headache. If you need anything, press the call button", the nurse walks out the door and back to the station on the ward next door.

The police officer stands up "Mr Richardson?"
"Yes" says James lightly
"I need to know what you remember about last night"
"Last night? I went to a pub with a friend, we'd watched the football match in the bar"
"Then what happened after the bar?"
"Nothing, I stood out the front, said goodbye to my friend and then turned to go to my car in the carpark, the next thing I know I was laying down with flashing lights around me"
"The paramedic said you kept phasing in and out"
"What happened?"
"You were mugged, from what we can tell someone hit you with some sort of weapon, possibly a bit of wood. A group of people from the pub heard you go down and found you laying face down in the car park. Can you check your belongings for me sir, let me know if anything is missing?"

On the chair next to the bed was a pile of clothes that James had been wearing. On the bedside was his wallet, keys and mobile phone.

"I should have another set of keys for the car" said James
"Was it a burgundy coloured Ford?"
"Yes, I think so"
"You didn't have the key, the bar staff found it on the floor under chair your been sat on earlier in the evening. I've already spoken to the hire car company and they are arranging to collect it"

James picks up his wallet and starts digging through it. Nothing is missing, there's even the £10 note he'd left in there.

"No, absolutely everything is here" says James
"Interesting, do you know anyone who'd want to harm you?"
"No, nobody. I mean I have money and there are those that are jealous but I try to be down to earth and not flash it around."
"OK, I will need to take a statement at some point, can I take

your contact details?"

James gave the officer his phone number and his two addresses. The officer thanked him and left him to get on. James wondered who he should call, they said whoever it is needs to be able to stay with him for 24 hours. He picked up his phone and scanned down the address book.

Hannah was on her lunch break at work when she saw it. A glance across the break room and on the TV in the corner that showed the news channel, a headline at the bottom of the screen. Local businessman hurt in attempted mugging. She sat transfixed as the presenter run through what little they knew, that James Richardson had been attacked by what is believed to be a single person from behind in a pub car park after a night out. They were about to move on to another story when they announced that the police had just released CCTV to help catch the attacker.

A grainy black and white image appeared on the screen. A group of people walked through the picture, then someone walked in from the bottom corner. As they walked towards a car, another figure walked out of the shadows all dressed in dark colours with something that looked like a baseball bat, they took a swing at the other person as soon as they hit the floor ran off. The group of people suddenly reappeared and one of them broke off and started running in the direction of the attacker.

Hannah looked back at her phone, one unread message from James, sent at 7:40 the previous evening. She stared at it for the longest time, wondering if she'd opened the message would it have made a difference? Just then her phone rang from a withheld number. She hated withheld numbers and was about to cancel the call when for some reason she answered it.

"Hi" came the voice down the phone "I'm nurse winters, I have a patient here who has given me your number as their contact for collection"

The Reunion Of A Lifetime

"I'm sorry, you must have the wrong number"
"Ok, sorry for bothering you"
"Thanks, bye"

Hannah hung up the phone. The pop-up reappeared, one unread message from James. She was about to open it when the phone rang again, again a withheld number.

"Hi, look I'm sorry you really have a wrong number"
"I've dialled it twice, I'm not sure I do" came the nurses voice
Hannah hears another voice faintly in the background "Let me talk"
"Hannah" James' voice comes over the phone
"James! I was just watching the news about you on TV"
"What and you didn't think to call?" said James sarcastically
"At least you haven't lost your sense of humour"
"No just some pride"
"I'm glad you're ok"
"Look, they are saying I need someone to stay with me for 24 hours and look after me"
"What, and you think I can just drop everything?"
"I wouldn't ask, but who else?"
"Your hordes of staff?"
"I can't really trust them with this, and I have no-one else to help me...Please"

Hannah thought about it, feeling guilty for not having opened the text, what else could she say.

"OK, I'll do it."
"OK, I'll put the nurse back on, she can explain"

The nurse explained the situation to Hannah and where to come to pick James up. Hannah hung the phone up and dashed off to her manager's office. She says that there was a family emergency, when pushed for further information by her manager she said "Look, I don't have time to explain. I will talk to HR about it when I'm back, but I really need the rest of this week off, take it as holiday or unpaid leave I don't care." Her manager was about to respond, but Hannah was already out the door heading to her desk to grab her coat and bag. She was in her car before she knew it and driving to the hospital.

Hannah walked into the room and was stopped in her tracks. James was on the bed wearing just his pants and trying to put a polo shirt on over his head.

"I'll wait outside" says Hannah
"Han? I need a hand" says James from inside the polo shirt
"I'll get the nurse"
"No...you can do it."
"Really? I can get a nurse"
"It's a waste of the nurse's time, I've already been too much of burden on them"
"OK, but don't expect me to be all Miss Nice Bedside Manner, because I really can't do that"

Hannah walked in and helped pull James' right arm through the sleeve. Then she looked up and saw it. From the front James looked fine, but from his right side you could see a huge purple bruise that went over his shoulder and up the back of his neck. No wonder he was struggling to lift his arm into the polo shirt.

"Thanks for coming Hannah"
"That's ok, I had nothing on really, just work" she said with a smile
"I will make sure you don't lose out on money you know"
"I know you will. Do you know what happened?"
"Not really, I left Rob outside the pub and went to the carpark and then I was here"
"I saw a video on the news, someone hit you with a baseball bat and then ran off"
"That explains the lump on my head then. Look, I don't like hospitals, too many sick people around. Can we get out of here yet? I'd like to get back to my own space"

The Reunion Of A Lifetime

"Let me go and check with the nurse"

Hannah went to the desk and spoke to the nurse, she was given painkillers and instructions to call the ward directly if James started to feel dizzy at any point or was nonsensical.

Hannah walked back in and said to James, "Let's go then Mr Victim". She walked him down to the car.

"Ok you're going to have to tell me where to go."
"You've got the address haven't you?"
"Yes, but I don't know where it is"

James gets out his phone and taps the screen. He puts it in front of him, a sat nav appears.

"Just follow that, it will lead you all the way to the underground car park" James pauses and smirks
"Carparked…absolutely" says James
"What?" says Hannah
"Completely roadsigned", James starts giggling to himself
"James? Are you all right?"
"Gazeboed!" James is in fully on belly laugh by this point
"James you're scaring me. Do we need to turn around?"
"No" said James between chuckles "it's a thing Rob said the other night"
"What on earth are you talking about car parks and gazebos?"
"Take any object, put ed on the end and it sounds like slang for drunk"
"Hmmm…Hosed…barriered…lamp-posted. I see what you mean" says Hannah

The rest of the drive is spent by them thinking up words to turn into names for drunk and giggling when they find good ones. Hannah turns the car into the underground car park, and pulls into the space next to James' car. She steps out of the car and walks around the other side. She opens the passenger' door.

"I don't need you to help me out you know" says James "I'm

more than capable"
"Sorry, I thought you were used to a chauffeur opening the car door for you." Hannah smiled
"Oh, ha ha ha" said James sarcastically. James got up gingerly and they wandered towards the lift to the house.

"Welcome to my understated little home" says James
"Bollocks is it, I've been here before" says Hannah
"I know, but could someone pretend it is a surprise, just once?"
"Come on let's get in"

James puts his key fob to the lift button and the doors open. They step in and the doors close behind them.

CHAPTER 15

Recovery and Discovery

The lift stops at the top and the doors open. They step out into the room that James describes as the vestibule.

"Vestibule, what a weird word, vest-eee-buouol" says James
"I think its probably french" says Hannah
"Probably, why are we standing in the vest-eeee-buuuullll?" says James
"Because you have the key for the door"
"Good point"

James takes his keys back out of his pocket and unlocks the door.
"OK let's go in", he says
He wanders through the door and heads straight for the sofa. Hannah follows him in and heads towards the open plan kitchen.

"Coffee?"
"Yeah, can do"
"How are you feeling"
"A little sore, and still got this headache"
"I'm not surprised"

Hannah starts digging around in cupboards and drawers looking for coffee. Eventually she opens what looks like a cupboard only to find a giant fridge inside it.

"I found the milk" she says, "any clue on the coffee?"

"Third cupboard along, top shelf"
"Why so far away from the kettle"
"Don't know, my mum chose where everything went when I moved in, she had her reasons"

Hannah carried on making coffee, whilst waiting for the kettle to boil, she looked at the bag of pills that she had from the nurse.

"Take as required to ease pain, no more than 2 in 4 hours and no more than 8 in 24 hours" it said on the label. She decided to withhold them until James needed them, after all, no use using up your allotted amount and then not being able to take them before bed and being unable to sleep.

"Do you take sugar?" asked Hannah
"Not normally" said James
"Might be good for you though, in this case"
"Why?"
"Like sweet tea for shock"
"Oh...just one then"

Hannah put some sugar in his coffee and came and sat on the giant sofa next to James.
James said "Do you want to watch some TV?"
"OK" replied Hannah, James passed her the remote. "Any preference?" she asked
"Not really, watch what you like, just not too loud"

Hannah started flicking around on the TV, she stumbled across the news.

"I take it you haven't seen this yet?" Hannah asked James
"No, not yet"

James' picture was at the top of the screen as the reporter repeated the story from earlier. The CCTV pictures appeared again, looking so much more vivid on James' giant TV, still grainy and black and white, but you could definitely tell it was James walking towards the car, then the figure appeared at the bottom of the picture.

James froze, "Han? I think I may have remembered something"
"What?"
"Suddenly I remember a smell, a whiff of women's perfume as I rounded the corner"
"What?"
"Women's perfume"

Something in Hannah sparks and she reaches for her bag, she opens her little perfume bottle

"Did it smell like this?"
"That's it!" says James "It wasn't you was it?"
"No, it was my perfume though! I think claire stole it from me. It could be Claire, or someone who wears the same perfume as me!"
"Can we prove it?"
"Not yet, all we have is a hint of a smell and I really can't believe even Claire would do that"
"I can, she's a prime bitch, why wouldn't she?" asks James

Hannah ponders the thought for a few seconds, the silence broken by another question from James

"Have you heard anything from Paul?"
"What? Since he turned up first thing yesterday morning demanding his clothes back?"
"He didn't!"
"He did, he was shouting up at the bedroom window, so I asked him where my perfume was. He pretended like he didn't know"
"So I pretended like I didn't know where his clothes were, closed the window and went for a shower"
"So you just left him outside"
"Of course, he knows where the supermarket is, even he could manage shirt and trousers at short notice"
"I've said it before, and I'll say it again, I never want to be on the wrong side of you." says James "Look, I'm going to have a sleep

for a bit, knock yourself out find something to watch or listen to, I have access to pretty much anything"

James snoozed on the sofa whilst Hannah watched repeats of old TV gameshows, some of which she hadn't seen since, well since she'd last seen James all those years ago.

James woke up at around seven o'clock, he could smell cooking. Peppers, onions, garlic, someone was frying vegetables, and given it wasn't him, it could only be Hannah.

"What are you doing" asked James
"Cooking" replied Hannah from the kitchen
"Really?" said James sarcastically "Seriously, what are you doing?"
"Making you dinner"
"What are you making"
"A surprise" says Hannah "you really do have so much food in this kitchen, I could make anything"
"Have you got anything for my head over there?"
"Yes, but you can't have them yet"
"What? Why not?"
"I think you should wait until later, otherwise you won't be able to take them when you need to when you go to bed"
"You're worse than my mum used to be"
"I miss your mum"
"Me too, what would she say if she could see us now?"
"I don't know, I hadn't seen her for years of course"
"I reckon she'd be glad, she always said she couldn't understand why we weren't friends anymore"
"I know, I'm really sorry about all that. You have no idea how much I regret hanging around with Claire at school"
"It's ok, we're past it now, aren't we?"
"Yes, we are. Now can you stop distracting me otherwise the food might burn? Watch some TV or something, I'll get on with this, it'll be around half an hour"
"OK, I'll leave you to it"

The Reunion Of A Lifetime

James picked up the remote and started flicking around the channels. He found an 80s music channel and put it on.

"I love this tune!" says Hannah "turn it up"
"There's a speaker on the counter in the kitchen, turn it on"
"I wondered what that was next to the kettle, but it didn't do anything earlier"
"That's because the TV wasn't on"
"Ah"

Hannah turned the speaker on with a click and then found herself dancing around the kitchen making the meal.

"I haven't had this much fun cooking for years" she thought

After a few minutes of dancing around and frying up food, she transfered the food to a dish and put the dinner in the oven. As she closed the door on the over, she spun away across the floor
"Don't fall over in there" says James, leaning against the corner of the cupboards
"No chance" says Hannah and she spins around towards him.
"How are you feeling" asks Hannah
"OK, I guess, sore head still"
"Care to dance?"
"What with my usual style and coordination?"
"Shut up", Hannah grabs his hand and drags him into the kitchen. A makeshift dance begins with them holding hands and spinning each other around across the kitchen floor. After a few laps James indicates that he needs to stop.

"I feel quite light headed now, and a little woozy" says James
"Are you ok, it isn't anything to do with your head is it?"
"I don't think so, I think you just spun me around too much"
"OK, well we'll keep an eye on it"

James went to sit back down on the sofa for a moment, Hannah started cleaning up all of the chopping boards and utensils from making the meal.

James was sitting there enjoying the music when suddenly Hannah called out
"Foods done, where do we eat?"
"We could eat at the table. I don't tend to eat there that often when it is only me" replied James, "I'll lay it"
"Thanks"
"What is it anyway?"
"I already told you, it's a surprise"
"I need to know what we need to eat it with"
"Knife and Fork, a sharp knife each I reckon. Do you have something to protect the table if I bring the dish out and we serve off of there?"
"I have a trivet somewhere!" says James
"What's that?" says Hannah
"A thing for putting hot stuff on, on a table"
"Oh"

Plates, knives and forks were all laid out on the table with the metal stand right in the middle of the table. Hannah told James to take his seat, so he sat facing the kitchen. Hannah opened the oven and a sizzling noise came from the dish that she removed and brought straight to the table.

"What is it?"
"Chicken with mixed mediterranian vegetables baked under a cheese topping"
"Wow!" says James "You managed to find all of that in my kitchen"
"You're kitchen is so well stocked, how do you not realise this?"
"I'm not here that often, I'm normally over a hundred miles away"
"So who does the shopping?"
"I phoned ahead on Friday and got someone to stock up for the weekend"
"Weekend? You could feed a village for a week with the food you have"

"Just as well they did as I wasn't planning on being here this long"
"No, well I'm glad you are" says Hannah

James started on his food.

"This is wonderful, you can cook this again!" says James
"Don't you go expecting this level of food every time, I'm not your chef you know"
"I told you, I don't have a chef. I normally do my own cooking"
"Yeah right, I bet you eat out most nights. Business dinners and the like"
"That's never been my style, I like my home comforts"
"OK, you'll have to repay me another day then, maybe you can cook at mine one night?"
"Sounds like a plan"

Hannah and James enjoyed their dinner and afterwards James took the plates from the table and headed to the kitchen. Hannah got up and headed for the sofa.

"Oh, you do your own washing up too?"
"Of course" says James. He turned and opened a cupboard door and it dropped down revealing a dishwasher.
"Well, when it is as easy as this, anyway". He put the plates and cutlery into the dishwasher and closed the door
"I washed all the cooking stuff up by hand, you didn't say anything", says Hannah
"You said to leave you to it, plus you seemed to really be enjoying it" says James

A cushion hurtled from the sofa over the counter and hit the wall in the kitchen.
"Hey, injured man here!" yells James from behind the counter.
"If it had hit you, you'd have deserved it"
James picks up the cushion from the floor and throws it back in the direction of the sofa without really looking
"Arrrggghhh!" yells Hannah

"What? Are you hurt?"
"The zip hit me in the face, it really hurts"
James dashes around the counter to the sofa where Hannah has her hands across her face
"I'm really sorry, are you OK?" says James
Hannah uncovers her face and smiles, she grabs the cushion next to her and smacks him around the face
"Got you!" shouts Hannah
"Ow!, don't forget I'm recovering from being hit over the head with a baseball bat" says James
"Oh, yeah", says Hannah ,"Sorry, did I hurt you?"
"No, not really" says James
"Good, I wouldn't wanted to have made it worse. You didn't deserve that last night."
"Oh, speaking of last night, did you get a chance to speak to Karen"
"Karen?"
"Yeah, did you call Karen about Rob? I sent you a message last night."
"Oh shit, the message" says Hannah, grabs her phone and opens the message, on the screen there are eleven words.

Do you think Karen would go on a date with Rob?

Hannah stared at it, the message she'd been so dismissive of, then so guilty that she hadn't read and it was the most innocent of exchanges.

"I haven't got around to it yet" says Hannah in a little lie.
"OK, well what do you think about it?"
"I don't know, I'm not sure if Rob's really her type"
"Well, the worst you can do is ask, she can always say no"
"I suppose"

Hannah got up from the sofa, walked over by the window and selected Karen's number. She held the phone to her ear.

"Hello" says Karen

"Hi" says Hannah

"Oh Hi, I've just seen the news, did you hear about what happened to James?"

"Hear about it? I'm here with him at the moment"

"Is he OK?"

"Yeah, a bit shaken up, but who wouldn't be"

"I guess, was that the only reason you were calling?"

"Well no actually. You know how you get these conversations that are my friend has this friend who likes you?"

"Yeah"

"Well my friend has this friend who likes you"

"OK, this doesn't sound weird at all"

"No it isn't"

"You're going to ask me to go on a date with a complete stranger, just because I mentioned I was single the other night"

"No, I'm not. Well ok, yes I'm going to ask you to go on a date with him but he isn't a stranger."

"Tell James, I always knew he used to stare at me and it creeped me out at the time. I'm flattered that he still feels that way but…"

"It isn't James" Hannah interrupted "it's Rob" the words hung in the air as the line went quiet for a few seconds

"Rob?" Karen said eventually "As in school Rob? He's a nice enough guy but…"

"Don't dismiss it. Yeah, Rob's a bit naive and maybe a touch of a kid, but his heart is in the right place"

"Why are you asking?"

"Rob told James that he liked you and somehow I ended up in the middle trying to play matchmaker"

"If I go out with him, it is on a few conditions" says Karen "It has to be a proper date with a proper restaurant, no fast food"

"Of course"

"He has to dress for the occasion, I don't want me in a dress and him in jeans and T-shirt, he's got to put the effort in"

"Obviously"

"And most importantly, he's paying. He strikes me as the sort of

person who's invite you on a date and then have just the bread rolls himself and go-dutch when the bill comes"
"I'll make sure he understands. So can I pass your number to James to send to him?"
"Ok, I suppose, look I'm going to have to go. Tell James I hope he is feeling better and we'll speak soon"
"Ok bye" says Hannah but Karen is already gone.

"Where's your phone?" asks Hannah
"On the table, why?" says James
"Just need to send Rob Karen's number"
Hannah picks up James' phone and starts tapping away
"Why can't I do that?"
"Because I can't have you involved, you have a bet riding on it"
She finishes what she is doing and passes the phone to James
"You deleted it!"
"What?"
"You deleted the message"
"Yes. Is that a problem?"
"Why would you do that?"
"So you don't try and interfere by calling Karen" says Hannah "Oh and Karen knows that you used to stare at her at school."
"I did not"
"Really?" Hannah's eyebrows raise up "I think we all noticed it. You were like some lost puppy watching her"
"OK, maybe just a little" James had gone slightly red in the face.

"Look, if you're feeling OK, I could use a little time alone" says Hannah
"You know where the room is."
"Are you going to be OK?"
"Yeah I'll be fine, only issue is getting my top on and off, but I'll probably just sleep in my clothes tonight"
"Don't forget to take pills if you need them before you go to sleep, not earlier"
"No Mum…" says James sarcastically

"OK, Call me if you need me"
"Will do"

Hannah headed off to the spare room feeling quite pleased with herself.

CHAPTER 16

Night And Day

Rob walked into the bar, and looked around, Tuesday evening, deserted. He wandered up to the counter.

"Hi Rob, here to settle your tab?"
"Not tonight, but I'll definitely sort it soon"
"Yeah right"
"Really, my mate has bet me that I won't get a date with a particular girl, and if I do he'll clear my tab for me"
"I'll believe it when I see it"
"Oh, you'll see it. Can I have a pint?"
"Have you got the money for it"
"Yeah, got paid this morning"
"OK"

The bartender pulls a pint of lager and hands it to Rob. Rob hands over the note and the bartender rings up the drink in the till.

"Nasty thing that happened last night wasn't it?"
"What happened?"
"Just after you left, some bloke got lumped in the car park"
"No!"
"Yeah, some rich guy apparently, probably someone after his cash"
"When you say rich guy, what do you mean?" Rob was suddenly quite panicky.
"He apparently owns a huge business up north, got loads of

money according to the news"

"Fuck!" says Rob and pulls out his phone. As he does, a message appears from James.

"Karen says she'll go out, but it's gotta be a proper date at a real restaurant, dressed appropriately and you have to foot the bill"

"OK, that's all right then. I thought you were describing my mate for a second" said Rob "but he's just sent me a text, so it can't be him"

"You were in last night with someone, weren't you?" said the Bartender "Where did you sit?"

"Yeah, me and James were sat over there" Rob gesticulated towards the table where he and James had sat the previous evening.

"Oh mate, it might be your friend. They found the guy's car keys under that table"

"Nah, like I said, he just messaged me, I'm sure he'd told me if anything had happened"

"Maybe" said the bartender

"Hey," said Rob "if I really wanted to take someone out for a good meal, I mean a really good meal, but without needing to wear a suit and tie, where should I go?"

"What? Suddenly money's no object to you?"

"Nah, I'm not paying for this, my friend is going to pay for it and get my tab here"

"Wow, some friend!"

"It's all part of a bet I've got with him."

"And you get a free night out and your over indulgent bar tab paid for? Maybe I should become friends with this person"

"Oi, leave out, he's not doing it for charity"

"Fair enough"

"Anyway, where's good?"

"I like that italian on the high street, always great food, but expect to pay a bomb for it"

"Like I said, not my issue"

Rob and the bartender spent the next hour sat at the end of the bar talking about the previous night's football match and which players were worth signing.

James was sat on the sofa watching TV, he was starting to really ache, and just wanted to settle down and snooze. He stood up with all intention of going to the kitchen and getting the pills. He started to feel a little light headed as reached out for the pills, the next thing he knew, he'd hit the floor.

Hannah had been sat on the bed reading one of the many books that she'd found on the shelf in the spare room when she'd heard the clatter in the kitchen and came running down the hallway.
"James!" she yelled and dived down on the floor next to him.
"I'm all right" James said softly
"No you're not."
"I am, I just got up a little fast"
"Really?"
"Really, I stood up a little fast and went light headed"

Hannah helped James to his feet.

"Well that settles it, I'm not leaving you on your own. I'm going to sleep in here with you"
"You can't there's only the sofa that you can lay on, and I don't want you to have to sleep in the armchair."
"OK, do you have any better suggestion?"
"Bedroom?"
"I suppose we could, we're both adults. What would the plan be?"
"Sleep in our clothes?"
"OK"

James picked up the box of pills from the counter, turned off the TV and led the way towards his room.

Sometime around midnight Hannah was lying on the bed looking at the ceiling, listening to James snore. *"How have I got myself*

The Reunion Of A Lifetime

into this?" she wondered. James had taken his pills and been out like a light as soon as his head had touched the pillow. Even with James facing away from her, his snoring was quite loud. Hannah was less comfortable than James. She had tried laying in different positions, she had dozed for a while, but now she was awake and staring into space. She started thinking about how she'd ended up here, everything that had happened since Saturday afternoon. What a whirlwind those four and a half days had been between meeting James, breaking up with Paul, arguing with Claire and James being attacked, her feet hadn't touched the ground. She certainly hadn't taken time to think about things properly, she certainly hadn't thought about her life without Paul.

When she'd met Paul, she'd been taken with him. He was the sort of person who would change their world for you. She was happy with her job but he had convinced her that she was good enough to look for a "better" job for more money. So she'd looked around and found another job, the hours were longer, the responsibility was huge and to be honest, not only was she scared of failing, she was working so hard she wasn't really having a personal life. Eventually she'd got into the swing of it, learnt to delegate roles and take back some control. She now had more money, and had bought her house. She didn't think twice when Paul moved himself in. The problem was, the job had made her a shell of herself, she wasn't happy and by now having Paul around was just habit. It was clear that Paul was happy to stagnate in the same job he'd been in for over twenty years and was expecting her to bring the money in. She was paying for a house that she could only just afford, all the bills were hers to sort, meanwhile Paul kept his money for his "expenses". It's only now, thinking about it that she realised how unfair this was and how Paul had maneuvered her into the breadwinner and homeowner whilst he was effectively freeloading, as he had done when he lived at his parent's house. *"I'm such a fool"* she thought to herself and began to sob.

James laid there, he'd heard Hannah sobbing, and he'd wanted to comfort her, but she'd been through a lot in the last few days and hadn't taken time out to grieve for the loss of her life with Paul. James thought it was best he didn't interfere. He laid there quietly trying to get back to sleep.

Eventually Hannah had managed to get to sleep, she woke up sometime later, daylight was starting to come through the curtains. *"Couldn't he afford proper curtains?"* she thought. She looked across at James, he was facing away from her and even in the dim light, she could see the purple bruise down the back of his neck. *"He doesn't deserve this"* she thought. She found herself thinking of James at school, James the outsider. He was the sort of person who everyone trampled on a bit and he was the butt of many a joke made by Claire. At most, some of the class considered him an acquaintance, but never a friend. Hannah worried that he would somehow realise that she'd let him down. She should have been there for him. How can she make right five years of ignorance and hurt, and twenty five years of silence since? Maybe that was why she was laying on his bed at this moment staring at him.

She looked at James' silhouette against the window. She laid there thinking *"He doesn't look half bad. He's toned up quite a bit since school. He was always cute"*. She was shocked, she'd caught herself checking out her friend. *"What am I doing?"* she thought *"He's just a friend"*. She turned over and settled down trying to sleep again.

James awoke, it was eight o'clock, his alarm was still half an hour away, yet he was awoken by something. It took him a few seconds to realise what it was. The feeling of a weight on his chest made him look down. Hannah had turned over and was snuggled into him with her arm wrapped over his body. Her head was nestled against his neck. James smiled, *"She must miss having someone in bed with her"* he thought. He closed his eyes again and waited for the inevitable alarm. "Beep, Beep, Beep" went the alarm, James opened his eyes, reached over and turned it off. Hannah stirred slightly and hugged him tighter. James felt himself relax into her arms. He felt safe with her.

Hannah subconsciously had squeezed in closer. Then it dawned on her *"Who is that?"*. She opened her eyes to look around James' room. *"Oh shit!"* she thought *"How'd I end up holding him?"*. She took her arm away and sat up, hopefully James hadn't noticed. She stood up and looked at herself in the mirror. *"I really need to get home and get myself washed and changed. If nothing else to get me out of my work clothes, and put a comfy bra on"* she thought.

James pretended to just be waking up. His head feeling much better this morning, he looked across at Hannah as she stood in front of the mirror he felt warm and fuzzy again.

"Checking yourself out?" said James
"Err…yes, and yes" said Hannah
"Yes and yes?"
"Yes, I was looking at myself, and deciding I look a mess and yes, I need to check out of the James hotel, go back to mine and myself washed and changed. If I'm going to be needed around here for much longer, I need to bring some of my stuff over."
"Like my clothes, makeup and phone charger as a minimum"
"Oh" said James "so you're not hanging around, only they did say twenty four hours and I make it only around sixteen so far."
"Well what are you going to do with yourself?"
"I'd better touch base with the office, prove I'm not dead"
"OK, you do that whilst I make breakfast, then you can come with me back to mine whilst I collect some bits"
"All right, I'd better brush my hair and look reasonable"
"Look reasonable?"
"Video call."
"Oh okay, if I can find everything will a cooked breakfast be ok?"
"Fabulous"
"I'll get out of your way then"

Hannah took herself off to the kitchen to prepare a breakfast. James wandered into the bathroom and brushed his hair. *"I look a proper mess"* he thought *"still I might get some sympathy"*. He walked down to the living room and picked up the laptop, and wandered off back to the bedroom with it. He put the laptop on the bedside and sat on the bed. He opened the video calling application and clicked on his second in command. The system had barely indicated it was ringing when the screen changed and he was looking at his vice president.

"James, how are you doing?"
"Fine thanks Nick"
"We all heard what happened, are you ok?"
"Reasonably"

He turned sideways on and showed his bruise towards the camera.

"Ooh, nasty" said Nick
"It looks worse than it is"
"Have the police caught anyone?"
"Not that I know"
"Were they after your money?"
"I don't think so, they didn't take any if they were"
"That's good at least"
"Maybe, anyway, how is everything going?"
"It's going fine. No problems, we just had the morning meeting, no problems at all"
"You're not just saying that are you?"
"No, there are the usual salesmen trying to push products through to make promises that they've made and we can't fulfil, but I'm keeping tabs on it all."
"Good, good. Nick, can you keep an eye on everything for the rest of the week? I don't think I should really be travelling like this"
"I thought you said you were fine?"

"I am, mostly, but I don't think I should be on the move just yet."
"Can I call you if anything comes up?"
"You can, but I'd rather you didn't, can't have me getting too stressed out apparently"
"Hey, no problem. Let me know what's going on, I'll keep an eye on everything for you"
"Cheers, speak soon"
"Bye"

The call hung up and James had managed to clear the rest of his week, that was five more days until he needed to be back in the office on Monday morning.

James got up from the bed and decided he needed a shower, he hadn't washed since Monday, it was now Wednesday. He got up and tried to remove his polo shirt, a little uncomfortable, but at least he'd got it off. He made his way into the ensuite and got himself undressed and into the shower. It felt good to be in the water getting himself clean.

Hannah had been working away, she'd found bacon and eggs and was well underway making a cooked breakfast, then she'd put sausages in a pan too, she'd diced potatoes and found tomatoes and beans, this was going to be good. The food was nearly ready so she placed the sausages and bacon on a tray under a low heat, and was ready to fry some eggs.

She went to check on James and call him for his breakfast. She walked into the bedroom, he was nowhere to be seen, she turned to walk back out and then she saw it, the ensuite door was open and James' outline could be seen through the frosted shower glass. She stood there staring at his form through the glass, it was only she heard the shower turn off, she snapped out of it. She made a dash for the bedroom door and as she headed back towards the kitchen shouted "Breakfast is nearly ready!"
"OK, give me 2 minutes!" yelled James from inside the shower.cubicle.

James reached out of the cubicle and grabbed the towel from the rail opposite. He dried himself and then wrapped himself in the towel, put on some deodorant and walked into the bedroom. He chucked pants, socks, jeans and even managed to pull a t-shirt on. He was feeling very positive as he headed off down the hallway.

Hannah was feeling flushed as she finished off making breakfast and plating up. *"What is wrong with me?"* she thought. Just then James walked into the room and sat down at the table.

"Smells delicious, what are you delighting me with this morning?"
"Besides my company? A cooked breakfast of sausage, bacon, eggs, beans, tomatos and potatoes. Sorry, the potatoes got a little burned, I got a little distracted", her cheeks flushed even more.
"Playing on your phone?"
"No, but that reminds me I need to charge it, its nearly flat"
"Oh, I'm sure I've got a charger somewhere for it, I have for most things"
"That'd be great."
"Are you ok?" asked James "You look like you're overheating"
"It's just being in the kitchen over the cooker, I got a bit warm" Hannah lied "How was your call?"
"OK, everything is going fine, so I've taken the rest of the week off to recover"
"Recover? You are looking like you are raring to go"
"I am, but what's the point of being the boss if you can't take a few days off. After all, you've already cleared the week with your work, haven't you?"
"Hmmm, I suppose. Did you put on your sick voice?"
"No, I was just talking softly and said that I shouldn't be travelling all that way until I felt a hundred percent"
"Liar! You're pulling a sickie"
"OK, you got me, but it was a good job I wasn't on the call still

when you shouted for breakfast"

"Sorry, I didn't think. I figured you'd be finished by then" Hannah lied to James again, knowing full well he wasn't on the call when she shouted out.

"No harm done anyway. I just don't want people thinking I'm taking advantage of the situation and your kind nature"

"You think I have a kind nature?" said Hannah, slightly taken aback

"Of course, you're wonderful, who else could I have called on to take care of me?"

"But what about school?"

"School wasn't about you and me, you were being harrassed by Claire. If anything I feel guilty for not saying anything, even if you wouldn't have believed me."

"Thanks, you are so nice to me"

"You deserve it. So what's the plan?"

"After breakfast, we head back to mine and I'll pick a few bits up. If we're going to be making the most of this week, I'm going to move into the spare room for the week. Enjoying the delights of Hotel James"

"Oh! Moving yourself in?"

"Just staying over for a few days, it makes it easier. After all, it's not like we have to be on-top of each other all the time, that room has everything apart from a kitchen."

"True, I suppose. OK, we'll eat breakfast and get on then"

They finished their breakfast and Hannah loaded the dishwasher. She ran a brush through her hair and got ready to go. James picked up his jacket.

"I guess we're taking your car" said James
"Why?"
"Because it's your car, and my driver isn't here"
"Sounds like a poor excuse, you could hire a car to drive us around"
"I could, but yours is here and anyway I'm injured"

"You look fine to me"
"What about this?" James pulled the neck of his t-shirt to emphasis the bruise
"Oh, are you going to milk this that much?"
"Well at least until the twenty-four hours are up"

They head out to Hannah's car. The twenty minute drive to Hannah's was mainly spent listening to the radio as James was engrossed in his phone. Eventually Hannah broke the silence.

"What are you up to on that phone? Not working are you?"
"Nothing, no"
"So what are you up to"
"None of your business"
"Are you working?"
"No"
"So what?"
"Hmmmm"
"Jimmy Jam?"
"OK, I'm playing Candy Crush, I've been addicted to it for years, it's my routine I always play it in the car on the way to and from work unless there's some emergency that I need to deal with"
"I did not have you down as a Candy Crush person"
"Shut up! I bet you play it"
"I do, as it happens, but I just didn't have you down for it"
"Well, I'm full of surprises"

They pull up outside Hannah's house. Hannah takes a deep breath.

"What's up?" asks James
"This place, it's full of old memories"
"It'll get easier"
"I know, but it isn't just the memories"
"What do you mean?"
"It was my house, but only because Paul convinced me to buy it."

"So what are you saying?"

"I'm saying, it's my house, but it isn't my home. I don't know what the answer is but it isn't this house"

"Take your time, think it through, obviously your breakup with Paul is raw"

"I knew Paul wasn't right, I've known for years and the truth is, this house was bought with him in mind. It's five minutes walk from his parents, ten minutes walk from his work, meanwhile my work is half an hour by car"

"I see what you mean"

"And until about a month ago, Paul didn't even drive. I did all the running around, still did until he got that cheap car last week. Honestly I thought the neighbours were going to have a fit when he pulled up outside"

"Was it bad?"

"The car was fine, apart from the fact that the paint was peeling, it had different coloured doors, was missing the rear bumper, smoked when starting from cold and occasionally backfired loud enough to wake the entire street up."

"So, you weren't popular then?"

"He wasn't, I made it very clear it had nothing to do with me"

"So where is it now?"

"Probably outside his parent's, you'd know if it was being driven nearby, you'd hear it"

They stepped out of the car and walked up to the front door. Hannah opened the door and they walked in.

"Make yourself comfortable" said Hannah "I won't be that long, I just want to get everything sorted and then we can get on our way"

"OK" said James and he launched himself across the sofa

"Hah, typical man, give him the option and he lays across the sofa"

"Of course, even if it did ache just a little to do it"

"Oh, poor baby!" said Hannah sarcastically "I'll be back down soon"

James turned the TV on and started flicking around the channels. He found a film on one of the channels that looked interesting. It was one of those brat pack eighties films that were all the rage. James had never got into them.
He'd been watching the film for around twenty minutes and an ad-break came on. That was when he realised Hannah hadn't come back downstairs. *"She's taking her time, just to grab some bits"* he thought.

He wandered out into the hallway, and called up the stairs "Hannah?". No answer came, he started up the stairs and made his way across the landing towards the bedroom.

"Han?" he called.

Hannah had planned to just grab bits and get going. But she realised that she was starting to smell and needed to freshen up. She'd popped back down the stairs softly and seen James watching the film on TV and figured she had time to grab a quick shower. So here she was in the shower when the knock came on the en-suite bathroom door.

"Han?" came the voice through the door
"James?" she answers
"OK, didn't know you were in there"
"Everything all right?"
"I was just checking where you'd got to"
"Needed a shower"
"Oh, OK" said James "I'll go back to watching the TV then"

Hannah thought *"It's a good job I've locked the door"* then she found herself wondering what if she hadn't. How would James have reacted given the same situation she'd been presented with earlier? *"Stop it"* she thought *"Get a grip, he's just a friend"*

She got herself showered and when she stepped out of the shower, realised there were only hand-towels left in the bathroom. *"No problem, I can use those to dry myself"*, she thought. So she dried herself with the tiny towel, and then had to get dressed. This presented her with her next problem. Her underwear was all in the dresser on the other side of the bedroom, with no towel this was going to be a mad dash past the bedroom door to get to them.

She opened the en-suite door slowly and looked around the door, James isn't in the bedroom, good. She shuffles out into the room and looks around the doorway into the hall. She can see down the stairs to the front door, James isn't in the hallway, good. She sneaks past the doorway and over to the dresser and opens the drawer. She is stood with her back to the door about to bend over and put her undies on when a wolf-whistle comes from the doorway.

"You still have a cute bottom" says James

Hannah freezes where she is, back to the door.

"James? What are you doing there?"
"Just nipped to use the loo"
"Errr, could you just nip somewhere else?" said Hannah keeping her back towards the door
"No problem, I was just saying, I mean I haven't seen your bottom since we were about five, so I didn't know, but it is very cute"

James walked back down the stairs to the sofa. To James this was a friendly exchange, he'd not been rude or seen anything else and had made a joke.

Meanwhile Hannah was mortified, James had seen her naked, at least it was only the back but still he'd seen her naked. Despite her obvious discomfort at being in the situation, the whistle and comment about her bottom had given her a warm feeling inside. She liked it when James complimented her, and she was starting to wonder just where was her head at.

Over the last few days, she'd caught herself looking at him in, assessing his body and looks. She loved it when he complimented her, she felt safe with him and had an unmistakable boost in positivity around him. Maybe it was nothing, maybe it was something, but she was just out of her relationship with Paul, she was still hurting, maybe that was it.

She got her underwear on and pushed the door closed, she proceeded to get dressed and collect up her stuff for her week away. She grabbed a suitcase from the stash under the bed, this one was smaller than the others, but the others were in hiding, holding on to Paul's clothes. She loaded the suitcase up and looked at it, that was most of her casual stuff in it. All she had left in her wardrobe were her work clothes and what she called her special occasions outfits. Special occasions were dining out at a restaurant, going out for an evening of cocktails or events like the reunion. She suddenly thought, she should take some of those and some going out shoes too, you never know James might want to go out for a meal one night. She grabbed her black dress and her black heels and draped the dress over the case. She went back down the stairs leaving the case and dress on the bed.

She walked into the living room as the film carried on being played out on the TV screen.

"I love this film" she said
"I've never watched it" replied James
"What? How can you not have seen it, it's a classic"
"Never been that bothered about them, they're so unrealistic"
"Yeah, but that's part of the point. It's all about escapism, and it's a love story. Love stories are supposed to be mainly fantasy"
"Hmmm...so do you want to get going?"
"Not yet, let's watch the rest of the film"

James sat up from laying on the sofa and Hannah sat down next to him. They sat there for the next hour at opposite ends of the sofa watching the film. At some point Hannah shifted over and

The Reunion Of A Lifetime

leant in to James' side and cuddled down on him. As she moved over, James sat there and put his arm around Hannah, because it seemed like the right thing to do. They watched the rest of the film, James being drawn into the story, Hannah loving it as she always does, even though she knows how it will end.

As the film finished, Hannah turned to James.

"Did you enjoy it?" she asked
"It was OK, I just knew how it was going to end after the first five minutes"
"Ah but it was the journey that kept you watching?"
"I suppose, I enjoyed watching it"
"What did you like about it?"
"Having my friend watch it with me"
"You're sweet, how have you not been taken up by someone?"
"I don't let anyone close enough?"
"Except me"
"Except you"
"Why?"
"I don't know, I suppose to start with I was so focused on my job, obsessive even. I never spent time with other people. Didn't take time to get to know people outside of work. Then when my uncle died, suddenly I had all this money and I was scared of being ripped off or taken advantage of. So I've never really trusted anyone since."
"Oh, so why do you trust me?"
"If I had to pick anyone to trust, who better, the person who has known me the longest?"
"But why?"
"You know so many embarrassing facts about me"
"You'd know just as many about me, so why me?"
"I guess, there's just something about you, I can't explain."
"So what, I'm special?"
"Quite, you're special"

They got up from the sofa and looked at each other

"You know what James?"
"What?"
"You're special too"

Hannah hugged James, James squeezed her back.

"Come on" said James "let's get back to mine"
"OK", said Hannah "you do realise that I'm bringing most of my wardrobe with me?"
"Ha, yeah right!" said James

Hannah went upstairs and grabbed the suitcase, the black dress and her black heels. She stood at the top of the stairs.

"One case? That's your whole wardrobe?"
"Well apart from my work stuff and my smart going out stuff"
"What's that?" said James pointing at the dress
"My dinner dress"
"For what?"
"For when you take me to dinner at an expensive restaurant"
"Oh, am I going to do that then?"
"Hopefully" Hannah smiles at him
"If you're lucky" he says

James dashes up the stairs and grabs the case.

"You bring your dress and shoes then" says James as he carries the case down the stairs.
"Great" says Hannah and heads down the stairs behind him. They go out of the front door and she locks up the house and they get into her car.

Paul has been at his parents for lunch and is walking back to work, as he rounds the top of the road he spots Hannah's car outside her house. *"That's odd"* he thinks to himself *"what is she doing home in the middle of a weekday?"*. No sooner has he thought it, than James and Hannah walk out the front door and get into her car. James is carrying a suitcase, Hannah is carrying her most expensive dress and shoes, the ones she got for a company party last year that Paul wasn't allowed to go to. He remembers, as he was really pissed off that it was employees only and no partners, especially when she bought the dress, she claimed that she barely ever had any spare cash to go out, yet here she was spending all this money on an outfit. Paul watched the two of them laughing and joking as they get into Hannah's car and drive off. Paul carried on walking past Hannah's house and onwards to work. He found himself asking various questions as he walked *"What had happened between them?"*, *"How long had she really known James?"*, *"Just how much money does James have?"*, *"Why can't he just fuck off and everything go back to how it was last week"* and most pressing of all *"What happened to all of my clothes?"*

As they pulled away Hannah thought she saw Paul walking down the road. It wasn't a surprise if he was, given his parents was one way and his work another. She didn't really have time to process it or check as she was driving away from the man on the pavement.

"James?" she said
"Yes?"
"Have you ever thought about the future?"
"What do you mean?"
"Life, where you want to be, family?"
"Not really, I haven't taken time out, you know that"
"I used to know what I wanted, now I'm not sure." said Hannah "I used to think a life with Paul would be great, but I can see it for what it was, a convenience for him"
"So what are you thinking?"
"I'm thinking, if I want a family I'm running out of time, I've wasted so long on Paul there isn't much of my life left"
"I hadn't really thought about it"
"You haven't got a family to pass the business on to even, have you?"

"No, there's no-one now"
"James? Would you mind if we stopped off somewhere on the way back this afternoon?"
"No, what did you have in mind?"
"You need some family, I want to show you someone who will be very pleased to see you"
"OK"

CHAPTER 17

The Other Woman

"Where are we going?" asked James
"You'll see" said Hannah
"I don't like this"
"But it's a surprise"

Hannah drove the car up the long drive towards White Lodge retirement home. It had taken nearly an hour to get here, but this was going to be worth it.

"Retirement Home?" said James
"Don't worry, you'll like this"
"You planning my dotage for me already?"
"Hardly" replied Hannah

They parked up and got out of the car. Hannah led the way into the front door and round into the day room.

Laura looked up from her chair, her daughter, Hannah, there in front of her looking brighter than she'd seen her in many years. She smiled back a thin smile, showing appreciation of her daughter being there. Then she saw him, the man walking behind her, this wasn't Paul, the miserable bugger she'd been with forever, this was someone else. There was something familiar about this man, she couldn't place it. The man smiled at her and held out his arms to hug her.

"Hi Laura" he said
"Hi...who are you?" Laura asked

"Mum" said Hannah "You know him"
"Do I?" said Laura
"Mum, it's James" said Hannah
"James?" said Laura, a gasp of realisation followed as she said "James!" and embraced the man in front of her. "I haven't seen you in what thirty years! Oh my haven't you grown?". Laura let go of James and turned to Hannah
"How did you end up finding James?" she asked "I thought you two were never going to speak again."
"A school reunion" said Hannah
"I see he's still getting into scrapes" said Laura looking at his neck
"That's a whole different story" said Hannah
"At least he didn't drag you into it like he used to" said Laura
"He was attacked in a pub car park a few nights ago" said Hannah
"Are you going to keep talking about me as if I'm not here?" asked James
"Sorry" said Laura "It's just such a shock to see you here. So what has happened to Paul?"
"He's a twat" said Hannah
"Hannah!" said Laura
"Sorry mum, but he is"
"I know that he is but you really should reign your language in" says Laura "you might offend someone. Anyway what happened?"
"Well, it's a little complicated" said Hannah
"He went off on one when Hannah hugged me" said James
"What? Why would he do that?" asked Laura
"I don't know, but then we later found out about Claire" said James
"Claire? What about her, did she start on you again?" said Laura to Hannah
"Sort of but that wasn't what pushed me over the edge, it was the fact that she used to be with Paul" said Hannah
"Fucking Bitch" said Laura
"Language Mother!" said Hannah

The Reunion Of A Lifetime

"Anyway, it didn't matter as Hannah slapped her in front of everyone" said James with a grin

"That's my girl" said Laura

"It's just a shame that James wouldn't let me hit her" commented Hannah

"Like I said at the time, she's not worth it" said James

"So you guys are obviously friends again" said Laura "I am so pleased. I always told Hannah she should get in touch with you"

"Mother" said Hannah

"Well, I'd always sort of pictured you two getting along. You were supposed to be together for life"

"Stop it Mother" said Hannah

"When you were kids I always thought you two would get married eventually".

Hannah went flushed in the cheeks. She wasn't really sure why, but this conversation was making her very uneasy. She smiled at James, who smiled back.

"Look, Laura, me and Hannah, we're friends." said James

"I'm allowed to dream though aren't I?" said Laura

"Of course, but we've only been back in contact since Saturday" said James

"Saturday? You've found James and booted Paul since Saturday?" said Laura in complete surprise

"Well actually, I decided to get rid of Paul the same night I met up with James. I threw him out the following day" said Hannah

"Why the following day? If you'd decided, why leave it to the next day?" said Laura

"Because…" Hannah paused before the completing the sentence knowing what her mother would think "…because, I spent the night at James' place. It isn't how it sounds…". It was pointless, her mother had heard the first sentence and was off.

"Spent the night at James'?" Laura turned to James, "Wow, you really don't waste time do you? I bet you loved it, my precious Hannah throwing herself at you?"

"Mother! It wasn't like that!" said Hannah
"Look, I think you've misunderstood" says James "she stayed in the spare room"
"Oh, so you haven't..." said Laura
"No" says Hannah
"...and you aren't..." said Laura
"No!" replies Hannah
"Oh," said Laura "sorry James, but you remember how protective I am of Hannah"
"How could I forget?" said James
"You clearly have a very low opinion of me though" said Hannah "to think I'd sleep with the first guy that came along"
"No, not at all, it's just well, it's James, it's not like you don't know him" said Laura
"I think I'd be much more comfortable if we got off of the subject of mine and Hannah's non-relationship" said James
"Me too" said Hannah
"OK" said Laura "so what do you do James?"

The next few hours flew by as they chatted about their childhood memories. Memories of James' mum and how James had become a millionaire. Eventually it was time for James and Hannah to make a move, they hadn't eaten since breakfast and still had an hour's drive back to James' place.

"It has been great fun" said James
"We must do this again" said Laura
"It's a date" said James
"And sorry again about misunderstanding earlier" said Laura "I suppose it was just some silly notion that I had in my head"
"Don't worry about it. As long as we never mention it again" replies James. James hugs Laura

"Take care" he said "you two are the only family I've got"
"You too" said Laura
"Bye mum" said Hannah as she hugged and kissed her mother
"I'll see you soon?" said Laura "Don't leave it so long next time"

"We won't" said Hannah

They turned and headed for the door, once they were in the car James looked at Hannah

"We won't?" asked James
"Well you know, I won't" said Hannah
"You said we"
"Well like you said, we're the only family you've got. You're going to want to stay in touch, aren't you"
"Yeah, you're right I guess"

Hannah pulled away and they headed off back towards James' house.

Rob stared at his phone again, Karen's number was on the screen. He'd been so full of bravado when he'd made the bet with James, but the truth was the next step scared him.

Rob had never done this, never made a planned move. He'd hit on girls in bars and the like but never approached them for a date, and certainly not sober.

He looked at the phone screen once more. He finally got the courage to reach down and press the button on the screen.

The phone the other end rang, then it rang again, then a third time, then a click and he heard Karen's voice

"I'm sorry, I'm not able to take your call. Leave me a message and your number and I'll call you back"

Rob pressed the hang up button on the screen. It was difficult enough to get the courage to phone her, but there was no way he was going to talk to an answerphone. He looked at his watch, quarter past three, she's probably at work. Rob started thinking, she hadn't mentioned what her job was on Saturday. She looks quite professional, maybe she works in an office in some high up job. Maybe she could get him a job, he'd like a steady income.

In the last few days Rob had seriously started considering what he was doing with his life. Meeting up with everyone else, who had a career or at least a permanent job and seemed to be making a success of them had got him thinking. What could he make a career out of. He after all has never really been trained for a career, bouncing from job to job. He had a great logical mind when he applied it, but had never really had the focus. He loved working with his hands and being productive, but every job like that he took on was a single task, like painting a fence. The job would end up getting repetitive and he'd get bored.

Even now, he was helping a mate hang some doors in his new house. They all needed to be cut down to size. Rob had thrown himself into the task at first, taking measurements and marking up each door in turn, but now he was on door number twelve and all this work with the saw had him getting bored. He'd only taken the chance to make a phone call whilst his mate popped in to make a cup of tea. Still just two more to do and then he'd be finished and have earned himself some handy cash to pay for his date until James came through with his part of the deal.

He his mate brought him a cup of tea. As he drank it, he couldn't help but wonder what Karen's response would be when he finally got to speak to her. It didn't matter that it made him nervous to take the first step, he wanted this date to work out and not just for his finances, but he really liked Karen. Rob found himself with a renewed determination after his drink to finish the job and get paid.

By the time he'd finished the last two doors it was gone six o'clock, but he was a hundred quid better off. He headed for the local pizza place to get some dinner with his money, but as he pulled up, he thought to himself that he'd better keep it for his date. He headed off home and got himself fish fingers and chips from the freezer and put them in the oven. Once he'd had his dinner, he looked at the clock in the living room, half past seven. She'd be home from work by now.

Rob picked up his phone and pressed the redial key on the screen. The phone rang, once, twice and then Karen's voice on the other end.

"Hello?" said Karen
"Hi Karen, it's Rob"
"Oh hi, Hannah said you'd call"
"Great, look Karen, I want to ask you something"
"Hannah's already explained, look I'm a bit tied up at the moment. I'm available tomorrow evening, just text me to say when and where."
"OK, well I thought we could go to..."
"Look, I haven't got time right now, text me can you?"

The line went dead. Rob was confused, that wasn't the way he was expecting that call to go. He went to send a text message, then some common sense kicked in. He looked up the telephone number for the italian restaurant. He clicked the call button on the phone's screen

"Hello, Marco's" said the voice on the end of the phone
"Hi, I'd like to book a table" said Rob
"Certainly sir, when for?"
"Tomorrow evening"
"I'm very sorry sir, we are quite busy tomorrow, maybe we could offer you a table on Monday evening?"
"No, it really has to be tomorrow"
"I'm sorry, but I haven't got any tables free"
"Nothing?"
"I'm sorry sir, nothing available"
"I had my heart set on your restaurant and it has to be tomorrow evening, I can't ruin this chance"
"I don't know what I can say sir"
"You see I've been waiting over twenty years to ask her out, and tomorrow is the only night she can do, if I don't do it then, I

don't know what to do"
"A romantic dinner, for two?"
"Yes"
"Twenty years?"
"Yes"
"One moment"

The line went quiet, no-one was on the other end and this carried on for over a minute. Rob was just about to hang up, thinking that he'd obviously just left the phone on the counter and got on with other customers, when a voice came onto the handset.

"Hello, I'm Marco" came the unfamiliar voice with a very strong accent
"Hi" said Rob
"My young friend said you need a table for a romantic dinner?"
"Yes"
"He said this meal has been waiting twenty years to happen"
"Yes"
"So why you leave it until the day before to book?"
"Errr…ummm…well I just asked her and the only day she is available is tomorrow"
"Don't worry, I'm joking" said the voice on the end of the phone, "I will find a way to add one more table for tomorrow night only, because I'm hopeless romantic, be here at half seven"
"Oh my, you have no idea how grateful I am"
"Just promise me you are here and you make most of the evening"
"Yes, yes, thank you"
"Can I take your name?"
"Yes it is Rob Crawfield"
"Mister Rob, this will be ready for you, seven thirty, no later."
"Thank you so much"
"See you tomorrow"
"Thanks, thanks, bye"

Rob hung up the phone not really knowing what had just happened. He quickly sent a message to Karen

"Meet me outside Marco's at seven twenty-five tomorrow evening x"

Just after he pressed send, he panicked, was the kiss too much? Would she agree? His phone beeped

"OK, see you then x"

Great thought Rob, then he looked at the message again, *"She's put a kiss too. That's very sweet of her"*, he thought.

He opened message application and wrote a message for James.

"Karen's agreed to a meal, you'd better get your wallet out!"

He pressed send, and then looked in horror at the screen.

"Message sent to Karen" it said in the middle of the screen.

"Shit!" he quickly forwarded the message to James, then opened a new message page
"Sorry Karen, sent message for James to you by mistake. James is helping me to pay for meal, I will pay him back"

"I think that's damage limitation done" thought Rob.

"No problem see you tomorrow night, x" came Karen's message

James and Hannah had just sat down to their dinner. James had made a lasagne. He was in a good mood and despite the obvious bruise, we already well past feeling ill effects of his attack. Hannah's phone beeped, a message. She decided to ignore it for now and enjoy her dinner. A few minutes later another message.

James looked at her and said "It's all right you know, you can check your phone"
"I don't like to, not during a meal"
"Really, two messages that quickly, maybe someone needs you".

Hannah's thoughts went back to the guilt over not reading Rob's message on Monday, even though it had no bearing at all on what happened.
"I'll just take a peek and see who they're from" said Hannah, she picked up her phone and swiped the screen. "It's from Karen, she says she's arranged to go out with Rob tomorrow, he's taking her to Marco's"
"Marco's, impressive, but then it is on my money" said James
"I'll say impressive, how does he get a Marco's reservation for the next day? They're normally booked about a week ahead."
"Who knows? Maybe he's offered to wash-up for a week?"
"There's another message from Karen, she asks me to call after nine, she has a favour to ask of me"
"Sounds ominous" said James

They return to their meal and then afterwards sit in front of the TV looking half-watching it as an old sitcom re-run is on the screen.

Eventually Hannah gets up and heads off towards the spare room.

"Where are you going?"
"I'm going to give Karen that call"
"Why are you going out of the room?"
"It could be private, I don't want you listening in"

She wanders into the spare room and closes the door. She picks up her phone and calls Karen

"Hi" says Karen
"Hi. So what do you want to ask me?" said Hannah
"Errr, well could you pop over tomorrow evening?"
"What? I thought you were out tomorrow evening with Rob"
"I am, look I'll explain everything when you get here, but I need to know if you can do this for me?"
"What?"
"Can you be here about six thirty? I'll explain everything to you

then"
"So what? Am I going to be the emergency phone call? You know the date isn't going well, rush in and tell you that you've got to come home quickly?"
"No, nothing like that, just please tell me you are about tomorrow evening"
"Yes, yes, I'll make myself available, I'm not at work this week, I've been looking after James"
"Tell him to come too, if he wants"
"OK, but you are being very secretive"
"I will explain tomorrow, thanks. Look I can't stay on the phone, I've got to go"
"OK, see you tomorrow then"
"Bye"

Karen hung up without waiting for Hannah's response. Hannah wandered down the hallway.

"That was odd" said Hannah
"What is?" asked James
"Karen, she asked if I can go over to her house tomorrow evening."
"Probably just wanted to make sure she looked nice, you know girly preparations for an evening out"
"Maybe, but it seemed like something more. Anyway, she said you were welcome to come over too"
"OK, that is curious."
"Are you up for it?"
"Going to Karen's house, yeah sure, why not"

The rest of the evening was spent in front of the TV watching re-runs of sit-coms, eventually it got to around eleven o'clock and James turned to Hannah.

"You're welcome to stay up, but I'm going to turn in" he said
"Me too, you certainly seem much better tonight"
"It's those twenty four hours, now they're over I feel much bet-

ter" he winked
"So I can sleep in my own room tonight?"
"Of course, it was you that insisted on sleeping in my room last night"
"I know, but I was worried about you"
"And you're not worried about me tonight?" said James with a wink
"Well you seem fine now"
"I'm just joking, don't take me so seriously"
"I know"
"Right I'm off to bed, I'll see you in the morning"
"Night night" said Hannah

James went off to his room and Hannah went to hers. James got himself undressed and went to bed, as soon as his head hit the pillow he was out like a light again.

Hannah meanwhile had unpacked her cases and got herself settled in her room. It really was like a home from home in the room. She spent some time pondering Karen's message, wondering exactly what she would want. Especially given she'd said James could come too.

Eventually she got herself ready for bed and settled down, she tried to get to sleep but her mind wouldn't stop going over the events of the day. She'd caught herself checking out James on multiple occasions and despite denying it, she'd spoken about her and James as we a number of times whilst talking to her mum. Just like James had said, she'd said that they wouldn't leave it so long between visits. What was going on? Was she thinking as her and James as an "us" or was there something else? She thought about how James had supported her when she threw Paul out, she thought about how James had called her for help and she'd come running. Despite all their years apart, within a few hours they were so connected and working on the same wavelength, it was like they'd never been apart.

CHAPTER 18

Making A Statement

Hannah woke up early, she'd been laying in the bed for quite some time trying to get back to sleep, but once she was awake, she just couldn't settle. He mind was still ticking over everything that had happened since Saturday and just wouldn't let her rest. Eventually she picked up her phone from the bedside, six o'clock, still early. She decided to turn the TV on in the room. She found very little on except for home shopping channels at this time of the morning or the twenty-four hour news channel, then she remembered that she could watch films on demand on the TV. She started scrolling around on the menu and found an old eighties film she liked.

While she was watching it, it started to bring her mind back to her time at school. Suddenly she wasn't watching the film, she was drifting through thoughts. The people she met and the places she used to go with Claire. It was only now as she played moments back in her head that she was realising just how all of Claire's friends seemed to actually just be being used by her or were scared of her. Hannah had enough academic ability to be useful to Claire when she needed help with school work. Her cousin Sarah who was basically a pro-shoplifter to order for Claire. There was Lisa who was a friend of Claire's older sister and used to buy bottles of cheap cider from the off-license for her. Stacey was Claire's gopher, if she wanted to do something risky, it was Stacey that did it for her. It was Stacey who got known for being the bad one. No-one on the outside of their little group ever knew that it was Claire that was pulling the strings. No-one inside the group would dare say anything against her, especially not Stacey.

Even the day Stacey was taken away by the police after some old lady saw her steal apples from a stall that she'd set up in her garden, Stacey didn't say it was Claire's idea. She didn't say Claire had threatened her until she did it. She just agreed to apologise to the lady and pay her for the apples that she'd taken. She'd taken the apples, and given the bag to Claire who'd taken one bite out of an apple, said it tasted disgusting and threw the whole bag over a wall into another garden. What a waste.

Hannah could feel the hatred starting to boil up in her again. She hated Claire for everything she'd put her through, but more than that she hated her for everything that she'd involved her in that had put other people through.

Hannah still remembers how her and Claire went their separate ways. Claire wasn't interested in Sixth Form but had some offer of a place at some technical college on the other side of town so soon after school they'd have no reason to ever meet.. Claire called her a few days after their exams were done and asked what she was doing.

"Revising" said Hannah
"Revising? For what?" asked Claire
"For the start of this course, it's a huge leap in difficulty from school to sixth form"
"But you'll breeze it, you always do"
"Hmmm, maybe"
"Well anyway, I'm going to the shops, meeting up with the girls. Gonna see if Sarah can get me a new outfit. Are you coming?"
"Nah, I'm going to stay here"
"I said, are you coming?"
"I said I'm staying home"
"No, you aren't, you're coming out with us"

"Look, I really need to do this"
"I'm not taking no for an answer, you need to join us"
"I'm busy"
"Fucking boring you are, you need to get out a bit, it's your final chance before college sucks all your fun out."
"Fine, I need to just finish this paragraph, give me half an hour"
"See, I told you, you need to be there"

Claire always had this way of just talking at Hannah until she agreed, and she knew it. However at that point, neither of them knew that this would be the last time they'd talk for nearly twenty-five years.

Eventually Hannah had got to the shops about an hour later, and was hanging around in the square in the middle of town waiting for the others to appear from whichever shop they were in. Hannah sat down on a bench opposite the large stone fountain that had recently been installed. She heard the commotion but it didn't dawn on her what was going on at first. She looked up and saw Sarah pelting out of the door of Debenhams with some t-shirt hanging out from under her jumper, followed quickly by Lisa who had a pair of trainers stuffed half in her pockets and Stacey bringing up the rear with some coat dangling out from under her own jacket.

Then she became aware of the alarm, and the security guard in pursuit of the girls. The three girls hurtled across the square. Sarah just kept running towards the fountain, she put her foot up on the side and jumped across the edge of the fountain, landing on the other side and keeping running. Lisa followed quickly behind and dived across the fountain with style. Stacey was never great at running, let alone climbing over stuff, she got to the fountain and as she stepped on the edge to follow the other two, she slipped and smacked the side of her head on the centerpiece of the fountain. Stacey collapsed into the fountain. The security guard went from being from the mindset of pursuit to that of first-aider in a second. He grabbed Stacey out of the water and laid her on the floor. He called for an ambulance from his radio. Stacey was bleeding heavily from the side of her head, and had managed to inhale quite a lot of water in the few seconds before the security guard had got there. A crowd had gathered around by this point, Hannah could no longer see what was going on. She did spot Claire sneaking out of the door of Debenhams, Hannah had looked straight at her and Claire glance, gave a knowing nod and then disappeared down the alleyway at the side of the shop.

After a few minutes, an ambulance arrived and the paramedics parted the large group to get through to the girl, they loaded her onto a stretcher and attached some sort of monitor to her and wheeled her into the back of the ambulance and disappeared off to hospital. Police were there too, they were asking on-lookers if they saw what had happened. Most couldn't really say, the whole thing had happened so fast. A group of young kids, could have been boys or girls, had run out of the shop being chased by the security guard. Some people thought that he'd caught the last one, some said that they thought he'd pushed her into the fountain. They asked Hannah whether she saw anything.

"I've only just got here, I'm waiting for my friends" was her answer.

Those words had haunted her. It was the evening before Stacey's parents had been found. Stacey had no ID on her, and no-one knew who she was. It was only when her parents had rung the police in desperation as she hadn't come back from meeting up with some friends, that they managed to work out who she was.

Hannah had tried to call Claire, but there was no answer that afternoon or evening. The following day Claire's mum said that Claire had suddenly decide to go away to her cousin's for the summer break and she'd let her know Hannah had called the next time she rang.

Stacey was in hospital for weeks, they were worried she may have brain damage and kept her sedated for the first few days. None of the girls had gone to see her, the rest of the girls had been keeping a low profile since their shopping spree went wrong and certainly didn't want to be associated with Stacey and risk being identified. When Stacey did come around, she said she couldn't remember the day at all. Hannah didn't go to see Stacey, she couldn't, she felt guilty that she hadn't helped her.

Eventually the police concluded an investigation into what had happened that day. Based on the statements of some of the people in the square, their opinion was that there was significant evidence that Stacey may have been pushed into the fountain inadvertently by the security guard. The police said it would be up to Stacey's family as to what happened next. They didn't press charges as Stacey clearly was trying to steal something at the time. That ultimately didn't matter as the security guard was relieved of his job, due to the bad publicity that the incident had afforded the company.

If only Hannah had spoken up, she could have helped someone who she thought of as a friend, made life easier for the doctors and the police, and ultimately could have saved someone their job. This was a guilt that Hannah had carried around with her since that day.

"That fucking bitch" thought Hannah, *"I've been loaded with guilt all these years, but she could've said something too. She could have told the police who Stacey was. Backstabbing little cow"*

Hannah was in tears, sat there on the bed, thinking of everything Stacey must have gone through. Everything that security guard must've gone through. How callous Claire could be to just walk away from it all.

The knock came at the door, followed by a gentle "Han? Are you alright?"

"No..." came Hannah's reply
"Should I come in?" said James from behind the door
"...Yes" came Hannah's answer between sobs

James opened the door. Dressed in his pajamas, he had a breakfast tray in his hands. He'd heard the TV on in the room when he'd got up and just decided to make a simple breakfast in bed option for her. Some cereals, some orange juice and coffee all on a tray. He wasn't prepared for what he saw. Hannah sat there in a t-shirt nightie crying her eyes out on the end of the bed was not what he'd expected to be greeted with this morning. He put the tray down on the floor and walked over to the bed and sat down next to her. He put his arm around her.

"Hey, hey, hey...what's up?" James asked
"Difficult to explain" said Hannah
"Paul?" asked James
"No...not Paul"
"Surely these tears aren't for Claire?"
"No"
"So what are you crying for?"
"For Stacey"
"Stacey?" said James "Stacey who used to hang around with Claire and you? What happened? Did you find out something, like she's died?"
"I've just realised I'm a really bad friend" said Hannah
"No you aren't, I'm friends with you, so you can't be that bad"
"You don't know about what happened to Stacey, do you?"
"What the whole security guard smashing her head open on a fountain thing?"
"That's just it, he didn't. Stacey slipped and fell"
"No one knows that for definite, that was just what the security guard said"
"I know, I was there"
"What? Why didn't you say anything?"

"Claire was ring leading them, she had her little group of mates out nicking clothes for her"
"So you were involved too?"
"No, I was late meeting them, they'd already gone in the shop when I got there"
"I saw it all unfold, I told no-one. Denied it to the police when they asked, and worst of all didn't even tell the police or the ambulance who Stacey was"
"They must've known, Stacey definitely had her parents with her, it was on the news"
"That was only when they reported her missing that night. I could have saved all that trouble"
"Why are you thinking about it now?"
"Sat her watching this stupid old film, dragging up all these old memories, memories that have all been stirred up in the last few days, I wish I'd never gone to the stupid reunion!"
"Don't say that!" said James
"Why not? That reunion has sent my life spiralling out of control. Before Saturday, I was a successful business woman, in a long term relationship, with a home and I thought I had it all. But, it turns out I've been lying to myself and the whole thing is actually a farce. Well I think sometimes ignorance is bliss."
"Hannah?"
"What?" Hannah snapped at James
"If it wasn't for the reunion, you wouldn't have met me again"
"I know," Hannah's voice had softened, "but the hurt of everything is getting to me. Realising me and Paul weren't meant to be. Remembering Stacey and the shop-lifting. But the biggest one was finding out Claire had been with Paul."
"Claire was with Paul long before you met him"
"I know, but there's a powerful AIDS poster in the doctor's surgery that I read once." said Hannah "It said something like, when you have unprotected sex with your partner, you are having unprotected sex with every other person they've ever had sex with"
"Urrrghh"

"Exactly, and for some reason that really freaks me out"
"So, how do we deal with this?"
"We can't that's just a part of history now"
"What about Stacey? Do you want to try and contact her?"
"What would I say? Hi Stacey, remember me? I saw you get injured and did fuck all."
"Hmm…So what then?"
"I just need someone I can talk to"
"You can always talk to me"
"I know, but you aren't always about. And what's going to happen next week when you go back to work and I'm back at my house?"
"Don't think about that now. We've got time until then. Have some breakfast" James hugged her into his side, and kissed her on the forehead, as he kissed her he glanced down and found himself momentarily staring at her cleavage
"Are you going to stop kissing my head?" asked Hannah
James realised he'd paused a little too long.
"Sorry", he said as he pulled away.
"Are you alright?" asked Hannah
"Yeah, fine" said James he paused looking away for a moment.
"Look what are we doing today?" said James
"I really don't mind, I don't want to waste the day"
"I know, I really should get in touch with the police and see if they have any progress. They said something about making a statement if I remember anything, so I probably should do that too"
"Well, I don't mind if you need someone with you."
"OK, I'll give them a call once I'm dressed, but let's have some breakfast first"

James turns himself around and crosses his legs on the bed. He starts pouring out cereal into the bowls in on the tray. Hannah turns to face him pulling her legs up and sits cross legged on the bed opposite him. As they eat breakfast, James tries to avoid staring at Hannah as he's feeling uncomfortable enough after staring at her cleavage. Hannah is also quite uncomfortable with James sat opposite her in t-shirt and boxer shorts, but they get through breakfast as best they can.

James heads off towards his room for a shower. He nips into the bathroom and is about to get undressed, when he remembers to close and lock the door. Not being used to having guests, he doesn't normally bother. He stands there looking at himself in the mirror. *"What just happened?"* he wondered *"Why am I trying to sneak peeks at Hannah?"*. He gets into the shower, thinking about everything that has happened in the last week. How Hannah became the person he would turn to. He has no idea who he would have called before the reunion if something had happened to him. He started weighing up his friendship with Hannah. There were definite positive points to her, she's known him since he was a kid, she was friends with him before he had money, she considers him part of the family and her mum loves him too. On the other side, he doesn't know where her head is at, she's just got out of a very one sided relationship with Paul and it is all so very raw, also he doesn't know how hanging around with Claire as a kid may have affected her. He switched back to the positives and thought back to his teasing her yesterday when she was naked at her house. She really does have a fine body, from what he saw from the back, and a fine set of breasts from the peek he took this morning. Suddenly he wasn't just thinking of Hannah as his friend, but he wondered if maybe there was something else. Was it just lust because he'd seen her naked and liked what he saw or was there some deeper feelings?

Meanwhile Hannah takes the opportunity to head off for her own shower in the ensuite. She ensures the bathroom door is locked, remembering both their incidents yesterday. She undresses and steps into the shower. Why can't her mind stop thinking about James? She keeps thinking of how nice he has been, and how he has helped her every step of the way this week. She also can't help but think of how handsome he is. From what she could make out through the frosted glass, he has quite a body too. She isn't sure, but from what he has said she doesn't think he's ever had a girlfriend. It's a complete waste of a wonderful man.

James is out of the shower and has got himself dressed in a pair of chinos and a polo shirt. He makes a phone call to the police station. The officer who he spoke to makes an appointment for him to come in this morning as the investigating officer will be in soon.
James heads off down the hallway to the guest room to speak to Hannah. He opens the door just as Hannah is straightening her dress.

"Hey!" says Hannah "You could knock or something, I might not have been decent"
"Sorry" says James "I wasn't thinking."
"What do you want?"
"I was just popping down to say I've got to go to the police station later this morning and make a statement"
"Oh cool, what time?"
"About eleven."
"OK, so before we go we'd better discuss everything and make sure you have your thoughts straight"
"Good idea"
"You go and make a coffee, I'll be there in a minute"

James wandered back to the kitchen and put the kettle on. He wondered if he'd walked in without knocking deliberately. After all, he normally stopped at the closed door. Before he knew it Hannah was stood beside him getting mugs out and putting instant coffee in them.

"So have you any idea what you are going to say?" asked Hannah
"Not really, I don't think there's much I can say."
"Well apart from what you remember"
"Obviously, but what information do you think I need to re-

member?"
"What time you got there, who was there, who you spent time with, when you left, where you went, also don't forget the perfume"
"The perfume?"
"You said you smelt perfume"
"Oh yeah, that's probably important"
"Probably? I think it is the most important thing"
"Really?"
"It might help identify the attacker"
"OK"

Eventually, they headed off to the police station, where Hannah went into the room with James as he gave his statement. Mostly it was straightforward until they got to the perfume.

"It was probably nothing," said James "but just before I blacked out I remember smelling a perfume"
"Really sir?" said the police officer "Can you describe it?"
"Oh, I can do better than that, Hannah has the same perfume in her bag"
"Really, can you please pass me the bottle madam?"

Hannah takes her perfume out of her bag and passes it to the officer. He takes a look at it and writes down the name of it.

"Expensive taste in perfume isn't it?" asks the officer
"I suppose, but it is one of the few luxuries I buy myself" replies Hannah
"I see, " says the officer "apologies miss, would you mind if I spoke to Mr Richardson in private for a moment?"
"Not at all" said Hannah

Hannah stood and walked out of the room, the officer checked the door was closed behind her.

"I have to ask you sir," began the officer "Do you think that your partner could have been responsible?"

"Sorry?" said James "Hannah? She isn't my partner"
"Oh sorry, I just assumed" said the officer "but do you think she could be responsible?"
"No, definitely not" said James
"Just so you know, I will have to review her as a suspect, just to rule her out"
"I don't think that is necessary"
"It is, you wouldn't believe how many times these stem out of domestic arguments"
"Like I said, me and Hannah, we aren't together, we're friends, we've only recently got back in touch"
"If you don't mind me saying, you seem very close"
"We've known each other since we were babies, she's like my sister"
"Ah, that's it then" said the officer "but I still have to investigate her"

James completed the paperwork and met up with Hannah in the reception area.

"He wants to speak to you now"
"Me, why?"
"Just to help with their enquiries"

Hannah walked into the room and there was an female officer in the room alongside the other officer who had been talking to James.

"This all looks very formal" said Hannah
"It is" said the first officer "would you mind taking a seat?"
"We just need to get some details from you at this point" said the second officer, "Where were you between seven and eleven thirty on Monday evening?"
"I was at home, alone, watching films" answered Hannah
"Is there anyone that can confirm this?" asked the female officer
"Not really, I was on my own"
"I see" said the female officer ", you have a very specific taste in

perfume."
"I know, I really like that particular scent"
"Isn't it odd that you and the attacker both wear the same perfume?" asked the male officer
"Not really, I had a bottle stolen from me the day before" replied Hannah
"Stolen?" said the female officer

Hannah spent the next half an hour explaining about Paul and Claire and the breakup and how she believed Claire had stolen her perfume. When she was asked for any evidence of Claire's involvement, she said she didn't have any. She did however show the officers the video of Paul in the garden and Claire collecting him. When they'd finished, Hannah gave the officers her contact details.

"Thank you Miss Waters" said the male officer
"I appreciate your honesty" said the female officer
"If you need me in the next few days, I will probably be at James' house" said Hannah
"Thank you for letting us know" said the female officer "I'm sure you understand that we must investigate all possibilities, and in most cases the attacker is known to the victim."
"No, I totally understand"

With that Hannah got up from the chair and left the room to where James was waiting outside.

"What happened?" asked James
"Oh, they needed to check I didn't try to kill you" said Hannah
"What?" said James "What made them think that?"
"My perfume, when you said I had the exact perfume, they thought maybe I'd done it"
"You didn't did you?" said James
"Of course not, but I think the police are on my wavelength and think it may have been Claire"
"Oh. Well let's get out of here, it's far too official in here for my

Carolyn Kemp

liking"

CHAPTER 19

Investigations and Discoveries

Claire sat at the dining table in her house. Claire was sat trying to work out what to do about Paul. Paul was nice and all, and he had his uses, but he had already proved to be a bit of a impulsive person, interrupting her chat with Hannah at the reunion. It was whilst she was pondering this, that a knock came at the front door. She walked to the door and opened it.

"Mrs. Wilson" said the taller of the two officers at the door
"Yes?" said Claire
"I need you to accompany me to the station"
"What? What for?"
"Either you can accompany me voluntarily, or we can do this another way"
"I don't know what you are talking about"
"Claire Wilson, you are under arrest under suspicion of the assault of James Richardson. You do not have to say anything. But, it may harm your defence if you do not mention when questioned something which you later rely on in court. Anything you do say may be given in evidence."
"What?"
"Come with me please Mrs. Wilson."

With that Claire was led out to a police car and taken to the station.

Paul was on his lunch break when he got the call.

"Withheld number, fuck off" and he tapped the ignore button

on the screen.

The phone rang again, withheld number again. He pressed the ignore button again.

It rang a third time, this time a number he didn't recognise on the screen.

"Persistent bugger aren't you" said Paul to the phone "OK, I'll answer". He tapped the green icon.

"Hello, Mr Taylor?" came the voice on the other end of the phone.
"Hello, yes?" said Paul
"Mr Taylor, I'm Inspector Davis at Winstone Town Police Station, I have Claire Wilson here who has given your details as someone to inform that she is currently at the station assisting us with our enquiries"
"What does that mean?"
"We will contact you in due course, but for the moment can you be available if required to pick Mrs Wilson up from the station?"
"Is she hurt?"
"No, nothing like that, as I say, we will be in touch"

The line went dead, Paul was left confused with just one thought *"Had something happened to Claire?"*

With no information Paul went back to work for the afternoon. His shift finished at five o'clock and he still hadn't heard anything. He was on his way to the car when his phone rang, Claire's number was on the screen.

"Claire?" said Paul
"Yes, it's me" said Claire
"What is going on?"
"Did you see that James was attacked the other day? The police took me in for questioning, they didn't any real explanation why but they thought I might have done it. Luckily I was out with friends on Monday night, so they managed to prove it

wasn't me"

"Wait, what? They think you attacked James?"

"Not any more they don't. Maybe because of the argument at the reunion"

"Are you still up for dinner tonight?"

"Yeah, can we meet there?"

"All right"

"I'll see you there"

"Bye"

"Bye"

Karen was in the kitchen when the doorbell rang. She dashed off to the front door and opened it.

"Hannah, James, come on in" says Karen

As James and Hannah stepped into the hallway, Karen looked nervous.

"You wanted to speak to me?" said Hannah
"Best to come through" said Karen

She led them into the living room, where a TV was turned on.

Karen turned to face James and Hannah

"James, Hannah, this is Leo, my son"

Karen held her hand out and a little boy got up from the sofa and grabbed her hand.

"Mummy, who are these people?" asked Leo
"They are my friends, James and Hannah"
"Are they nice?" asked Leo
"Well I think so" said Karen
"Hello Leo" said Hannah
"Hi" said James
"Hello" said Leo, "Mummy, can I go back to my programme?"
"Of course" said Karen

Leo ran back to the sofa.

"Wow" said Hannah "So this is what you wanted to talk about?"
"Sort of" said Karen
"So how old is Leo?" asked James
"He's four"
"Five next week!" yelled Leo from the sofa
"Yes you will be" said Karen back "Come on, let's go and talk in the kitchen"
Karen started to lead Hannah and James through to the kitchen
"I think I remember this programme from when we were kids. Do you mind if I stay and watch the TV while you two chat?" said James
"Really?" said Karen "All right. Just don't ask Leo about it, you'll never stop him. Come on Hannah, let's go and chat"

Hannah takes a seat in the Kitchen and Karen goes to turn the kettle on.

"Drink?" asks Karen
"I'm not really in the mood for a hot drink. Do you normally drink coffee at this time of day?" asks Hannah
"Most of the time." replies Karen "It keeps me going, you would not believe how much energy having a child around takes out of you"
"Fair enough, so is Leo what you wanted to discuss?"
"Kind of" replies Karen "You know Rob don't you?"
"Only a little, I haven't spoken to him since school apart from the other night"
"But you guys were friends at school, weren't you?"
"He was a hanger on, but yeah we got on. Why?"
"Do you think he's responsible?"
"Rob! Responsible? No chance"
"Hmmmm...that's what worries me"
"Worries you? You're only going on a date"
"I know, but I have to think about Leo. Is the person I date going

to be right for him"

"Woah, aren't you thinking a bit ahead?"

"I don't want to get involved with someone only to have to let them go as they can't cope with a family"

"No, of course not. Can I ask you the obvious question?"

"What obvious question?"

"Where does Leo's dad fit into this?"

"Oh, over three-thousand miles away and doesn't care"

"Wow... What does that mean?"

"He lives in the states and sends money every month for me to help with Leo, but he wants nothing to do with him. We both agreed our short lived relationship was a mistake, and I got pregnant. I'm not blaming anyone, I knew the risks, but at least Leo's dad agreed that he had to make financial contributions"

"So it has always been just you?"

"Since Leo came along, I haven't dated anyone. Never got the time. Being a single mother has taken all of my life up, but recently I've started to let go. The girl next door has babysat Leo a few times and I've been the theatre or cinema with friends. Last week he stayed at my Mum's for the reunion and I had the best night out I can remember."

"Wow, so no man, and no dating since Leo came along."

"Nope"

"I'm sure Rob will be fine, go out have fun, make sure he knows about Leo early on. Then it'll be his decision whether to man up or if he can't cope. Put the ball in his court early, then before you get emotionally attached you've both got the chance to split"

"Small problem with that"

"What's the problem?"

"I think I really like him. We spent quite a bit of time together at the reunion."

"It'll be fine, like you said, you don't really know him. If it isn't working out, you can leave it. You could even decide just to be friends"

"I suppose..." said Karen, clearly not convinced

"Look you are strong, you have made this all work, haven't you? With a kid around and doing everything by yourself that's got to have been tough"
"Oh it has"
"How do you make ends meet? You have a lovely house by the way."
"Oh Thanks, obviously Leo's dad sends me some money but I make most of my money selling on auction sites online"
"What? So what do you sell?"
"Whatever I can find reliably and cheaply in bulk. Last week I bought a crate of fifty electric tin openers. Sold them all separately and more than doubled my money"
"How do you get time?"
"Selling is online, you can do it whenever. Normally in the evening when Leo is in bed. I'm always here to take deliveries during the week, and a courier collects my packages when I book them in"
"Wow, a proper business empire from your house! Does it really make that much money though?"
"I've paid for the house off of it. It is a bit risky at times, especially with technology, you have to know the warning signs before you buy. I once got scammed on a load of new games consoles, but it was my own fault"
"Oh, what happened?"
"I misread it. A crate of new boxed games consoles, was actually a crate of new games console boxes"
"Subtle difference"
"Yeah! You don't know anyone who needs a box for their games console do you?"
"No…surprisingly" said Hannah sarcastically.

Just the the doorbell rang.

"That'll be Anna, here to look after Leo"
"That's probably our cue to leave anyway, you need to finish getting ready"

"Hannah, thank you for coming over. I just needed to check before I go and make a fool of myself"
"That's fine"

The doorbell rang again.

"Oh shit" said Karen as she ran back to the door and opened it "Sorry Anna, deep in conversation."
"That's okay Karen", said the teenager stood in the doorway. She looked at Hannah as she walked out of the kitchen. "Hi" she said to Hannah
"Hi" said Hannah

Hannah walked past the pair in the hallway and looked into the living room

"James, we need to let Karen get ready, we need to get going" said Hannah
"Just a second" came James' response

There is James sat on the sofa with his mobile phone in his hand showing videos to Leo

"This new version of the show is rubbish, I was just showing Leo the classics on YouTube" said James
"They're cool" said Leo
"Smart kid" said James
"We really need to get going" said Hannah
"Alright" said James
"Oh" said Leo disappointedly "you'll come again one day?"
"You betcha", said James
"Don't worry" said Anna from the doorway "I'm sure I can get them on my phone too"
"Yay!" shouted Leo
"Look I'll see you soon Leo, you're cool" said James
"You're cool too, James" said Leo

James and Hannah headed to the door.

"Looks like you've made someone's day" said Karen
"I just couldn't let him keep watching those poor imitations of a cool programme" said James
"I think you've got a friend there" said Karen
"Give us a call if you need anything" said Hannah
"Will do, thanks again"
"You're welcome"

James and Hannah left and Karen closed the door.

Hannah watched James as she followed him back to the car.

"Never really had him down as the playful fatherly type, he has been so wasted" she thought to herself.

CHAPTER 20

Date Night

Rob was stood outside the restaurant. He glanced at his watch just after twenty past seven, "Good, here in plenty of time" he thought. Just then his phone beeped "God, I hope she isn't cancelling on me". Rob pulled his phone out and looked at it, a message from James. He tapped the message.

"Are you at the restaurant?" said the message on screen

Rob tapped away

"Of course, you think I'd be late for this?!" he replied.

Karen stepped out of the taxi and looked across the road. She wasn't sure who she was looking at to begin with. *"A man wearing black shoes, smart trousers and a decent shirt, that can't be Rob can it?"* she pondered *"it is!"*

Rob looked across the road, he could easily make out Karen getting out of the taxi, she looked stunning in her dress, just like she had done at the reunion the other night. He watched her as she crossed the road towards him.

"Hi" said Rob
"Hey" said Karen and she lent over and kissed Rob on the cheek.
"Where are we eating?" she asked
"At Marco's" Rob replied proudly
"Marco's? How long have you been planning this?" asked Karen
"I rang them yesterday"

"What and they had a table available?"
"Well, not for just anyone." said Rob "I know Marco, we had a chat on the phone and he agreed to make room for us"
"You...know Marco?" said Karen slightly confused "How?"
"Oh you know how it is. I do odd jobs, I'm always connected to someone. There's that whole six-degrees of separation thing"
"Hmm..." said Karen "...why are we waiting out on the street? Shall we go in?"
"Okay", said Rob and he held open the door and let Karen walk through first.

"Name?" said the waiter stood by the door
"Crawfield" said Rob "Rob Crawfield"
"Ah yes, Mr Crawfield, Marco's special guest" replied the waiter, "This way sir and madam"
"Wow" thought Karen *"He really does know Marco."*

The waiter led them through the main restaurant and out towards the back, they went past a door to the kitchen and through a door. They suddenly found themselves outside the back of the restaurant in a little walled garden. There was a table in the middle of the garden with candles on it and two places set. The waiter held out a chair for Karen to sit on, she proceeded to take her place. He then walked around and held the chair out for Rob, who took his. The waiter then handed them both a menu and a wine list. Rob took a look at the wine-list and then turned to Karen.

"Do you want to pick a wine?" he said "I'm always rubbish at picking one and normally get the one that isn't quite the cheapest"
"Are you sure? Do you prefer red or white?" asked Karen
"I don't mind, I'll drink either, so it is completely your choice"

Karen looked down the menu and ended up ordering a rosé. Whilst the waiter was getting the wine, Karen asked Rob a pressing question.

"Are we having starters?" she asked
"Do you want starters?" replied Rob
"I don't mind, are we having a three-course or just main?"
"We might as well go the whole hog"
"Are you sure? it could work out expensive"
"Yes, I'm sure. I may not have much money, but I want to have a nice night with you, so I've pulled out all the stops, and some favours"
"I can see that" said Karen

The waiter brought the wine and poured them each a glass. He left to give them a few minutes to decide which dish they wanted from the menu. As the waiter disappeared through the door, a short man came the other way.

"Roberto!" shouted the man "So glad you came." The man walked over and hugged Rob, which took him a little by surprise but he went with it. The man turned to Karen.
"And you must be the lady I have heard all about." he said "Known each other over twenty years and this is your first date, yes?"
"Yes" said Karen "You must be Marco"
"The one and only!" replied the man "I just wanted to check everything is alright, I tried to fit the table but there was no room inside, then I remembered out here and thought you'd like it out here."
"It's lovely" said Karen
"Wonderful" said Rob
"Okie-dokie, well I leave you two to it. You need me, tell the waiter to fetch me, otherwise enjoy your evening"

"I really didn't think you'd pull this off" said Karen "But this is definitely a good start"
"Did you doubt me?" asked Rob
"I just didn't think that you'd go to this level"
"I wouldn't normally, not for anyone else" said Rob

Karen felt taken aback by this comment. Was it true, or was it just a line Rob was spinning? She didn't know. Just then the waiter reappeared and took their order. Karen knew that if she was to stick to her plan, and check Rob's commitment early, she needed to get started soon. So once the waiter had gone, Karen got out her phone and put it on the table next to her.

"So Rob?" she started "How have you really been since school?"
"Fine, you know, just fine"
"I know you aren't in a relationship at the moment, but any serious relationships?"
"Woah, that's a bit personal, isn't it?"
"Well, I'm just trying to get up to speed. Let's call it speed-dating life history"
"Well, ok, nothing too permanent on the job front of late. No really serious relationships. Most of my girlfriends only lasted a few months then for one reason or another we'd split up."
"Any particular reasons?" asked Karen
"No nothing that I can really remember. Apart from Sally, she suddenly took a job in Mexico about five months ago."
"Whilst she was dating you?"
"Yeah, apparently she'd totally forgotten she'd applied for it and was then offered it and decided to go," replied Rob "But, I'm sure I saw her in Tesco the other week"
"Really"
"Might've been a trick of the light, as next time I looked, she was gone"
"Maybe"
"But nothing serious, no ex-wives on the scene?"
"No, why do you ask?"
"Because I have something like that"
"What? An ex-wife?"
"No, but I come with baggage"
"What are you talking about?"

Karen picked up her phone and flicked through the camera gallery.

"This is my son Leo" said Karen as she handed the phone to Rob
"Your son?"
"Yes, my son"
"Is it important to you that I know about him?"
"Of course, what if you didn't know about him and we started seeing each other. It'd be a shock if you turned up at my house and surprise! Here's a four year old I've never mentioned that takes up all of my time"
"I still don't understand"
"Does it make a difference?"
"Does you have a son make a difference to what?"
"How you might feel about me"
"Karen, we're both in our early forties, there was always a chance that one of us would have some sort of baggage. I'm not stupid you know. And no, it doesn't make a difference to me. If I like you and we get serious, then why would it make any difference. He's part of your life, I can make him part of mine too if that's what it takes"
"If that's what it takes?"
"To be with you. I suppose that sounded wrong, what I meant was I'd be glad of the opportunity to be part of his life too"
"Oh, so not the roadblock that I was thinking it was"
"You thought this would be a problem?"
"Of course. Leo is wonderful, but who wants to take on someone else's kid?"
"We are getting a bit ahead of ourselves here, we haven't even got our starters yet"
"No I know, but I was talking to Hannah and she convinced me that I needed to know if you were prepared to be part of Leo's life before I got in too deep."
"No, not at all"

Just then the waiter appeared with their starters. As they sat and ate they began chatting about their relevant lives. Karen talked about her home sales and even told the games console boxes story to Rob.

"I'd have listed them myself" said Rob
"I can't do that, I have a reputation to uphold"
"As long as you aren't misleading anyone, I bet you can shift them"
"Maybe"

Rob then went on to tell his story about how he got fired from the newsagents.

"That's so wrong" said Karen
"What is?"
"Doing that, helping them steal stuff"
"But where else were they going to get it? The internet wasn't around then was it?"
"I know, but you still shouldn't have let them steal it"
"I can hardly turn around and ask them for money for a hidden mag can I?"
"Still, I suppose you're heart was in the right place, even if the execution was rubbish"

They had a lovely meal and had just finished their main course when Rob announced that he needed the toilet.

"Don't do a runner on me" said Karen
"Would I?" said Rob
"I wouldn't put it past you" said Karen with a smile.
"I'll hurry back, just don't eat my dessert if it gets here before me"

Rob wandered into the toilet and when he'd finished doing his business and washed his hands, he looked at himself in the mirror.

"You've got this" he said to himself

Just then a cubicle behind him opened and someone walked up

The Reunion Of A Lifetime

to the sink next to him. Rob glanced across and was sure he recognised the face, but couldn't place it.

"Everything alright pal?" Rob asked the familiar stranger
"Err, yeah"
"You look a little unsure"
"It's nothing, just a secret I'm keeping from someone"
"Secrets are never good, it is a woman?"
"How did you guess"
"Guys don't get cut up over other guy's opinions so it had to be. Look whatever it is, talk to her about it. You never know, she could be supportive."
"Yeah, right, I suppose"

The stranger finished washing and drying his hands and left. Rob stayed staring at himself in the mirror.

"I so want this" he said to his reflection "Can I do this? Can I be that person? Only one way to find out I suppose"

With that Rob turned to head out of the toilet. As he opened the toilet door, he could hear the screaming coming from the restaurant. A woman somewhere was going thermonuclear at their other half. Instead of instinctively heading for the door to the garden, Rob turned towards the main restaurant. It was then that he realised what he was looking at.

The stranger from the toilet was in a full blown argument with Claire in the middle of the restaurant.

"YOU'RE A COMPLETE PRAT AREN'T YOU!" yelled Claire
"What? No! I was trying to protect us and do what we'd agreed"
"BY GETTING ME ARRESTED?"
"I didn't plan on that happening no"
"GET OUT OF MY LIFE YOU IDIOT BEFORE YOU RUIN ANYTHING ELSE!"
"Claire, no, you're all I've got"
"BETTER FIND SOMETHING ELSE THEN!" she continued.

Within seconds she'd grabbed her coat and headed for the door.

The man slumped back down in his chair in the middle of the restaurant. The noise died back down and he just sat at the table as everyone else tried to just go about their business. Rob turned and made his way back towards the garden.

"Everything alright? You were gone ages" said Karen
"Yeah, I think I've just seen the most bizarre scene in the restaurant"
"Oh yeah, do tell what got you so distracted from your dessert."
"I just saw Claire from school having a right argument with someone in the middle of the restaurant"
"I thought I could hear shouting"
"I'm not sure who the bloke was who she was screaming at, but apparently he got her arrested"
"Claire, arrested, that'll be the day. She never did her own dirty work, always got someone else to do it"
"Maybe that didn't work this time. She definitely said that he was the reason she had been arrested. The thing is, I have the oddest feeling I've seen him before, but I can't put my finger on where from"
"I'm sure it'll come back to you"

Karen quickly taps out a message to Hannah. "Did you know Claire had been arrested?"

Her phone beeped with a response almost immediately

"No. When? What for?"

Karen replied, "I don't know. Rob overheard her arguing with someone in the restaurant about how they'd caused her to get arrested"

"Interesting" was Hannah's response

Karen and Rob ate their desserts and then Rob went and spoke to the waiter away from the table and sorted out payment. Karen wasn't sure what the deal was, but Rob clearly had some sort of arrangement going on. Rob returned to the table.

"I've had a wonderful evening", he said
"Me too", said Karen
"So what now?" asked Rob
"I need to think about getting back to Leo"
"Fair enough" said Rob "I'd like to meet up again sometime"
"Of course, not too soon, I have to arrange a babysitter and make sure I can pay her"
"I was actually thinking, next time we could all do something together"
"All? What including Leo?"
"If you want. Look you having a kid isn't going to scare me off. I enjoy spending time with you. If it doesn't work out, I'm sure we can still be friends and hey I was a boy once, you know. Maybe I can help you with Leo"
"OK" said Karen "Let me know what you want to do and when, and we'll see if we can fit into your busy schedule."
"It's a date"

With that Karen stood up and her and Rob left the restaurant. Out on the pavement the taxi was waiting for Karen.

She turned around to Rob and said "I really enjoyed this evening"
"Me too" said Rob. Karen leant towards him and he went to turn his cheek so she could kiss it, but she followed his lips and gave him a full on kiss. Rob was shocked momentarily, but then kissed her back.

"I'll see you soon, give me a call" said Karen as she turned and got into the taxi. Rob just stood there with a grin on his face as the car pulled away.

CHAPTER 21

Looking Back And Making Plans

Rob headed off home with a buzz in his head. He'd drunk a fair bit of alcohol but for once that wasn't the reason for this buzz. He'd just kissed Karen.

The thing was Karen was one of those unobtainable girls at school. She always gave the air of having a boyfriend, but was never seen with anyone. It wasn't just James that had found her alluring at school. It had turned out most of the boys had thought of her at some point or another. Rob more than most it turns out. He lived for the moments that she'd smile and say hi in the corridor, he used to daydream about her whilst working at the newsagents and he definitely used to think about her when lying in bed at night, wondering what it would be like to kiss her soft lips. He loved those lips, whenever she spoke he would watch them intently. Now he'd kissed them, and it was everything he'd anticipated and more, not least because she'd kissed him too. He could never have believed that she would ever been interested in him.

So here he was back at home, sat on the sofa with the TV on at two in the morning trying to find something boring to distract him from the fact that his mind was racing. He flicks through the TV guide talking to himself.

"Crime drama, no"
"Old gameshow, no"
"80's uk sitcom, rubbish"

Just then his phone vibrates. He looks at the screen a message from Karen.

"Thank you, I had fun tonight, xx"

He sat there looking at the message, smiling.

"Me too, didn't think you'd still be up" he tapped out and sent.

The phone went again a few seconds later.

"Can't sleep, mind won't settle"
"Me either, watching rubbish on TV"
"You shouldn't do that, it'll keep you awake"
"Almost as much as using your phone"
"I know, I'm going to get a hot chocolate"
"Good idea, I may join you"
"You'd better stay at yours ;-)"
"You know what I mean"
"I was joking"
"I know :-)"
"I really should try and get to sleep. Leo will be up around 6"
"6! that's early"
"That's normal for him, unless we have somewhere to go early, then you don't see him until 9."
"OK, I will let you go and try and sleep. I will send you a message tomorrow about another date, how are you fixed for Saturday?"
"Nothing planned for Saturday, let me know"
"Will do, xx"
"Look forward to it, xx"

Karen looked at her phone. Why had she entered into a conversation like that? There was no way she was going to sleep now. She was curious what Rob had planned for Saturday.

As Karen turned to sit on the bed with her hot chocolate, she spotted it on top of the wardrobe. A cardboard box that she'd almost forgotten about. She put the hot chocolate down and reached up for the box. She placed it on the end of the bed and opened the top of it. Inside there were various keepsakes from her life. Trinkets from family holidays, a story book she loved as a kid, a photo of her mum from when she was little and there was what she was looking for, a pile of books, each with a different coloured pattern on the front and a sticker. She took the books out of the box and placed the box on the floor.

She looked at the first book, on the sticker in the corner was neat curly writing.

Karen's Diary - Book 1 - Started 1st January 1990

She drank her hot chocolate as she flicked through the pages looking for the entries she knew were in there. She eventually found them

~~~~~~~~~~~~~~~~~~~~~~~~~

Sunday 6th May

Left home this morning at 8 to make the long drive to our new house. It's nearly 4 and we've only just arrived. Mum is rushing around making sure that we've all got somewhere to sleep tonight. It's so unfair, being made to move. My friends are all still back at home and I'm here. Mum says it'll be home soon enough, I'm not so sure. Oh and Mum just said that I'm going to school tomorrow. New school, I hadn't even thought about it. I haven't had to be the new girl, ever. I just know it's going to be horrible. I hate it all.

Monday 7th May

Didn't sleep well last night. This house smells funny, I think the last people had a dog. I kept hearing noises, mostly cars going past, but it is so much busier here than at home. At home, at home, Mum keeps reminding me that this is home now. It isn't, she doesn't understand, just keeps telling me to give it a chance.

On the plus side, school wasn't too bad. It was just as awkward being the new kid at school as I thought it might be, but luckily some of the girls are okay and showed me around. There was one girl called Hannah was nice, but everytime she spoke to me another girl in the class scowled at her. There was also this boy called Rob who kept making jokes. I asked Hannah about him, she said he's always like that. I think he's quite cute, maybe he fancies me?

Tuesday 8th May

I don't know what I've done. Hannah was horrid to me today, I thought yesterday we were starting to become friends, but she was so mean, and her friend Claire just kept smirking at me. Rob keeps making jokes still. Still not sure if he likes me, or if he really is just a bit of a joker. I like the attention from him though, he makes me smile.

~~~~~~~~~~~~~~~~~~~~~~~~~

Karen sat staring at that last sentence, it was so true, he really does make her smile. She thought about how lovely he'd been this evening and found herself wondering if she should have given him a chance at school. The truth was she never gave anyone a chance, not at romance. She'd always managed to convince them that she had a long distance relationship with someone from 'back home', the real truth was she'd seen what her Mum went through with her Dad and didn't want anything to do with a relationship.

She downed the last of her hot chocolate, hugged her diary to her heart and curled herself up on the bed. She slowly closed her eyes and started to drift off to sleep, her mind full of the image of Rob smiling at her.

"Mummy, mummy!" came the loud voice waking Karen from her dreams.
"Mummy? Mummy! I missed you last night" said Leo
"I missed you too, honey" said Karen groggily.
"What's this book, Mummy?" asked Leo

Leo had Karen's diary in his hands and was looking at the coloured cover.

"It's very pretty Mummy, can I have it?" asked Leo
"I'm afraid not, little boy. This book is Mummy's and it is very special" said Karen
"What is special about it?" asked Leo
"It is called a diary. It is a special book where you write something about what you have done or how you are feeling every single day"
"Is it a story?" asked Leo
"Sort of, I used to write in it every day when I was a little girl. I wrote what I'd been doing, who I liked, who I didn't, what music I listened to, what was on TV, all-sorts of things."
"Wow, can you read me it?"
"I'm sorry, a diary is so special because it contains feelings that only the person who wrote it should know about, so you never let anyone else read them"
"But I wouldn't read it, you would be reading it to me" said Leo cheekily
"I'm really sorry, these books are mine, and I don't like others hearing what is in them. Maybe we could make one for you"
"Don't be silly, I don't write"
"I know, but you could draw a picture for each day, to remind you of what you did"
"Yay" said Leo "Can we do it now?"
"Give me a chance, we need to get dressed and have some breakfast first"

An hour later, Karen is sat at the table with a cheap A4 drawing pad with a sticker on the front of it that says 'Leo's Diary'

"OK Leo, it is ready"

She holds it up to him and shows him the sticker.

"This is Leo's Diary" she says

The Reunion Of A Lifetime

"Yay! Can I start now?" asks Leo
"If you want"

Leo sat at the table for hours drawing and colouring a picture. Karen went about her housework, momentarily checking her online auctions and updating prices where things seemed to have slumped off. Eventually Leo got up from the chair.

"I'm done!" he said

"What have you drawn?" asked Karen as she walked around to look at the sheet. There were clearly two adults standing and an adult and a child sat on the sofa.

"This is yesterday. That is you and Hannah, and this is James and that is me. James is holding his phone for me to watch." said Leo
"Wow, that is amazing" said Karen "I'm very impressed. Did you enjoy making it?"
"Yes, I want to keep my drawing book forever, just like you keep your writing book. Mummy, can I watch TV now?"
"OK, but not for too long"

Karen looked at the picture. She took a snap of it on her phone and wrote "Someone made a big impression" as a comment and sent it off to Hannah as a message.

"Is that Leo's drawing? That's so cute" said Hannah
"Of course it is. You didn't think it was mine did you ;-)" wrote Karen
"Ha, ha, ha, of course not" came the reply
"It is the first page of Leo's diary"
"Diary?"
"He saw my old diaries and we decided he could make one. But as he doesn't read or write, his are going to be pictures"
"Wow, he is quite talented. Was going to message you, I've been waiting for the gossip. How did last night go?"
"Surprisingly good"
"What about the whole situation with Leo"

"He's being very grown up about it. He said, everyone our age has some form of baggage, and he has no problem with it"
"But is that just him being nice?"
"No, I think he really wants to make an effort and be part of Leo's life"
"How can you be sure?"
"He said he wants both to go out with him somewhere tomorrow"
"Wow, where?"
"I don't know yet, I'm not sure he has any idea, but he seems keen"
"Did you find anything more out about Claire?"
"Only what I said last night, she had an argument with someone about her being arrested"

James wanders into his living room and finds Hannah engrossed in her phone.

"Candy crush?" he asks
"No, messaging Karen actually" she replies
"Ah yes, the date. How did it go?"
"It sounds like it went really well"
"Bugger, I guess I'd better pay up then"
"I guess so. Oh, and Leo has drawn a picture"

Hannah shows James the picture on her phone.

"What is it?" asks James
"It is you and Leo watching your phone on the sofa"
"How sweet"
"Apparently it is the first page of his picture diary"
"He's a nice kid, very intelligent for his age"
"Not like you were at that age then"
"Charming!" said James
"Just saying, you were stupid at five years old"
"No I wasn't"
"You got yourself stuck in that tree in the garden, didn't you?"

"That was really scary"
"Yeah, right up until the moment you screamed like a girl and your mum came running out into the garden."
"Do you know what is the most embarrassing thing about it?"
"Other than your screaming?"
"I didn't realise at the time that the branch was only about four foot up"
"See you were stupid" said Hannah with a grin
"Were, that implies that you don't think I am now"
"Well, you have your moments"
"Good to see I have your full support" said James sarcastically.

James took out his phone and sent a message to Rob.

"OK mate, sounds like you had a good evening. I guess I need to pay up."

The reply came back a few minutes later.

"Yeah, I can't tell you how great my night was. I think I may have finally found someone I can really connect with"
"That's nice for you, just don't go leading her on" replied James
"No chance, I want this to work"

James looked up from his phone and turned to Hannah

"What are you doing tonight? Any plans?"
"Nothing in particular, I thought we were hanging out together"
"I know, but I thought maybe you'd be bored of me by now"
"Not really, why?"
"I need to go to the pub and settle up Rob's bar tab, so I thought I might meet him there."
"What? At the pub where you were attacked? Is that wise?"
"I think so, I think whoever attacked me knows that the police are looking for them. They're not going to try anything stupid."
"I suppose I could go back home tonight" said Hannah trying not to sound too disappointed "Make sure the pipes haven't burst or something"

"Maybe you could have a girly evening with Karen"
"Maybe, it'd be good to go back home and check everything out at least."
"Do that first, then go to Karen's? She'll have to put Leo to bed at some point"

James looked back at his phone.

"Shall we meet tonight?" he sent
"OK, Where?"
"The pub again?"
"As long as you don't go getting yourself beaten up again"
"No chance, I'll have my ninja skills on, see you at 7:30?"
"OK"

Hannah was busy on her phone

"Can I pop over later?" she sent to Karen
"Yeah sure, what time?"
"I was thinking 8ish, maybe I'll come by taxi and bring a bottle with me?"
"Alright, but text first to make sure Leo is off to bed"
"Sounds good"

Rob was standing in the car park of the large Zoo that was just outside the town.
"I hope they like animals" he thought to himself as he walked in to reception.

"How can I help you sir?" asked the bubbly girl behind the counter.
"Errr, well I want to come to the Zoo tomorrow, but I don't want to have to wait around. I've seen those queues at the weekend and I'm not sure queuing for over an hour is going to be much fun."
"Certainly sir, you can purchase tickets in advance or you can purchase one of our passes that allow you to come back for a whole year."

"How much is a pass?"
"It works out just over the price of 2 day tickets but you can come in any day except christmas day for a whole year"

Rob looked at the price list. It was pretty expensive. A few of those passes would set him back more than last night's meal would've, but he decided it was worth it.

"2 adults and a child pass for a year" he said
"Do you want them to start from today?" asked the receptionist
"No, tomorrow, please"
"That's fine"

She took payment and gave him a gift ticket to bring in the following day with which to get the passes once inside the Zoo. He sent a message to Karen,

"Picking you both up at 9:30 tomorrow morning, is that ok?"
"OK, what are we doing?"
"It's a surprise"

CHAPTER 22

Evenings In And Out

It was five o'clock as Hannah walked up to her front door. She'd left James at his to get ready for his night out with Rob. She opened the door slowly as the post got caught under the door from the other side. She closed the door and picked up the post from the floor. A few bills, a couple of bits of junk mail and a handwritten envelope.

She opened the envelope and looked inside. A single sheet of paper was in there. She unfolded it at began to read.

Dear Hannah

Before you tear this letter up, please read it fully.

I didn't know what else to do. I've made a terrible mistake. I didn't mean to be so jealous at the reunion, you were there hugging him and then you said everything to me. I was confused, I went outside for a breather and bumped into Claire.

Claire always had control over me. Within minutes she had made me see red and think you were having an affair with James. I know now that you weren't and I'm sorry that I ever thought that of you.

And yes, I did something wrong that night. I brought Claire back to ours, but nothing happened. We just chatted, we slept on the bed, but I promise you I didn't have sex with her.

I'm sorry, can you take me back?

Your once beloved,

Paul

Hannah stared at the letter. No feelings, no remose came, just anger. She was so angry at this letter because it only just scratched the surface of what was wrong. Yes, it was apologetic, but he also made excuses and didn't approach the deeper issues. He is lazy and doesn't trust her. Far from winning her back, this letter just pushed her away. She started thinking about Paul and how he was on Sunday, treating her like everything was her fault. He could be such an impulsive, petulant child sometimes.

"Oh my word!" Hannah said out loud to herself "That's the link"

She picked up the phone and made a call.

Paul was on his walk home from work when his phone went. A text message from Hannah. Maybe writing the letter had worked.

He'd had the idea after Claire left him in the restaurant. He'd realised that Claire didn't care about him, just what he could do for her. He also realised that without Hannah and Claire, he had nothing. He was back living at his parents. *"I'm forty-two, who lives with their parents at forty-two?"* he'd thought. An act of desperation, try to remember what he'd done wrong and apologise, maybe he could win Hannah back, get back on track to where he was just a week ago. He'd written the letter this morning and posted it on his way to work.

He opened the message.

"Thank you for your letter, it reminded me of so many things about you..."

"That's a good start" he thought

"...such as how heartless you can be. You were a complete arsehole to me last weekend, but it isn't just about that. You've been taking me for granted for ever. Did I ever ask you to move in with me? Have you ever paid for anything to do with the house? You are a lazy, useless, fuck. Do not call or text me again and stay away from my house."

"Bugger" thought Paul

He carried on walking home, he took the alley that went through the back of the housing estate, not wanting to risk walking past Hannah's, she was clearly pissed off, and being too close might be risky (although at least this time he had his clothes on!). It was as he approached his parents that he was met by a car coming the other way.

A man got out of the car and wandered over towards him.

"Mr Taylor" said the man in front of him
"Yes"
"Can you come with me?"

The man flashed a badge in his wallet at Paul. A police officer, this could mean only one thing.

"Of course" said Paul
"If you'd like to get in the back of the car please"
"Certainly"

Paul stepped into the car and waited as the officer got back into the driver's seat. Paul was resigned to what was going to happen from here on out. His fight all but gone after Hannah had rejected him.

James was just putting jeans and a t-shirt on when his phone rang. Unknown number, it said on the screen. James answered it tentatively.

"Mr Richardson?" came a voice
"Who wants to know?" replied James
"I'm calling from the police" said the voice on the end of the phone

"Oh, then yes, I'm Mr Richardson"
"This is just a quick call to let you know that we have arrested a gentleman for the attack on yourself, and he has admitted it was him"
"Oh, that's good. Wait, you said a man?"
"Yes"
"What about the perfume?"
"What about it?"
"I'm sure I smelt perfume just before I was hit"
"We are going to conduct an interview with the gentleman shortly, but I assure you, we think it was definitely him. I can't say any more at this moment"
"Well, thank you very much anyway for the update"
"We'll be in touch soon"
"Bye"

"Well that's a relief" thought James, *"at least I don't have to worry about them still being out there."*

Rob sat down at the bar, a smile on his face

"What's got you so happy?" asked the bartender
"A couple of things. You're going to be happy in a few minutes" said Rob
"Oh yeah, why's that then?"
"Because my bar tab is going to be cleared"
"What? You're going to pay it?"
"Yep"
"All of it?"
"Yep"
"Never!"
"Actually, you're right I'm not going to pay it"
"I knew you were winding me up"

James walked in the door at this exact moment. Rob turned to see him in the doorway.

"I'm not winding you up" said Rob "I'm not going to pay you, he

is"
"What?" said the bartender
"Hi" said James to Rob
"Hi" said Rob

James looked at the bartender and said "I'm here to settle a tab for my friend here"
"OK, give me a second" said the bartender. He pulled out the book and a calculator and started adding everything up. I think it's three hundred and one pounds fifty."
"Shall we call it three-ten?" asks James "Just in case you've made a mistake"
"OK, cash or card" asks the bartender
"Oh, cash, always cash if you're paying off a tab"
"Great"

James handed over the money and the bartender put it in the till.

"Now" said James to Rob "What are you drinking?"
"Not too much tonight, I'll have a pint with you, but no more"
"What, why?"
"Got to keep a clear head, going out at nine thirty in the morning"
"Where are you off to so early?"
"Picking up Karen and Leo, going to the Zoo. Did you know Karen had a kid?"
"Yeah, he's a nice lad. Seems very intelligent"
"Good, hopefully he'll like me"
"I'm sure he will."

James turns to the bartender "Two pints of lager then please"
"Certainly sir" said the bartender
"Put it on my tab!" said Rob
"Fuck off" said the bartender "I don't think you're ever getting another tab"
"Hopefully shouldn't need one" says Rob

"Oh yeah" said James "Why is that?"
"Going to get myself sorted, get a proper job"

They take the drinks and James pays for them. They go and sit down at the same table that they sat at on Monday evening.

"Get a proper job? What's brought this on?" asked James
"I suppose it was the reunion, everyone having someone or something going on and there I was just bumming along. I need to make a success of something"
"So what are you looking to do?"
"I don't know, something office based would be nice. I've always had to do practical jobs. Painting, decorating and the like are fine, but what I like is the planning of a good task, understanding what is needed and where I'm going to get the stuff from."
"Interesting, I might know exactly where there is a job for you, but not just yet, it's a few weeks away"
"Anything would be good. Something I can make my own would be nice"
"Oh you'll definitely have a chance to make it your own if this comes off"
"Any clues?"
"Not yet, let me see if the idea has legs before I get everyone's hopes up"
"Everyone's?"
"Yes everyone's. I think there is a place for you and Hannah in my business, and even possibly Karen, but her availability is limited."
"You've got to be careful, mixing friends with business"
"I know that, but I can trust you guys."
"So why don't you trust me with the idea?"
"Because I haven't finished working it all out yet"

Hannah got out of the taxi and walked up to Karen's front door. She sent a message from her phone to let Karen know she was outside. A few moments later Karen came to the door.

"Thanks for that, I didn't want Leo hearing the doorbell and getting up" said Karen
"That's fine, I brought wine"
"Oh goody, You go through and I'll get some glasses"

Hannah walked in to the living room and sat on the sofa. Karen reappeared with wine glasses in her hands.

"So, how was last night?" asked Hannah
"Oh my god, it was amazing. Marco's is lovely, and the food is mindblowing" replied Karen
"I wasn't talking about Marco's, and you know it" said Hannah
"I know" said Karen with a smile "But it was lovely. Did you know that Rob knows Marco?"
"No he doesn't, does he?"
"They seemed quite close, he came outside and hugged him and everything"
"Outside? Marco met him and you on the street personally?"
"No, Marco had setup a table for us in his garden area"
"What garden area?"
"I don't know, it was around past the kitchen"
"Marco's own garden?" said Hannah "Wow!"
"I know, and we had a wonderful meal out there"
"Enough about the restaurant, how was Rob?"
"Well I told you earlier"
"I know, but I thought that given time, you might think differently about it"
"No way, I really like him"
"Really? Rob"
"Yeah, the truth is I always have"
"Really?"
"Yeah, look at this"

Karen walked to a unit and pulled out her diary, she flicked to the relevant page and handed it to Hannah.

Hannah read down the page through the entries. Eventually

Hannah looks up.

"Oh Karen, I'm so sorry. I was such a bitch" said Hannah
"Don't worry about that part, I've long since forgiven you for what Claire did to you. Did you see the bit where I said I like him, he makes me smile?"
"Yeah, I saw that, so you really have had a thing for him all this time?"
"I suppose" said Karen with a smile
"Since your first day at school?"
"At least a little bit."
"That's so cute." said Karen "Do you think that he's serious?"
"I really do, he has a surprise trip out booked for me, him and Leo tomorrow"
"That's nice of him. Any idea on what he has planned?"
"None at all. I'm sure it'll be fine"
"Really? You don't think he's planning sky-diving then?"
"No, he's a good guy. He really does seem to have his head screwed on underneath his jokey outside"
"Are you sure?"
"Yeah, I think he's really is sensible underneath it all"
"OK, well then I'm happy for you. Anyway, shouldn't we start on this wine?"

James and Rob left the pub after just one pint. On the way home Rob had an idea and popped into the supermarket. He collected everything he would need to make a picnic for the trip tomorrow. When he got home, he spent over an hour making sandwiches and preparing everything. He made sure he had cool packs in the freezer, this was going to be a great day.

When James got in, he went to his bedroom and grabbed his laptop. He set it up in the kitchen and started digging through his files. He found the stuff he wanted, the plan for the reunion. He spent around three hours in front of the laptop tapping away.

"It'll work, I just need the right people in the right places" James

said to himself.
"What will?" came Hannah's voice from the doorway
"Hannah? What are you doing here? I thought you were staying at yours tonight?"

Hannah and Karen had spent a couple of hours chatting away about Rob and Karen's meal, and Hannah told Karen all about Paul's note and how it wasn't going to be enough. She explained how he'd always been selfish and how she felt that she was only there as a convenience to him when they were together. All the time they were talking about Paul, Hannah couldn't help thinking about James. How different her time with him was, how he respected her and didn't treat her like an idiot, how she felt completely comfortable to talk to him about anything. They'd got on so well all week, despite how long they'd been apart.

When they'd finished the wine, Hannah and Karen said their goodbyes and Hannah headed for her house. When she opened the front door. She looked around, the house was similar in design to Karen's but all she could think was her house felt cold. She compared it to the feeling she got at Karen's house. Karen's house was warm, friendly, inviting. Her house was cold, functional and felt like it wasn't hers. It was like a show house, on the surface it looks fine but there was no love here. It was her house, but it wasn't her home. There was only one place that felt like home right now. She called herself a taxi.

CHAPTER 23

The Grand Plan

Hannah didn't say anything at first, so James repeated his question.

"What are you doing here, Hannah?"
"I needed to be with a friend, you don't mind do you?"
"I suppose not, it was just a bit of a surprise"
"So what were you talking about? What will work with the right people?"
"A new business venture"
"New business venture? What kind of business venture?"
"I suppose you need to know, especially if I want you to commit to be part of it."
"What? Me?"
"I know how good you are at organising and planning your work. I only had to check your profile online to see how highly work colleagues regard you"
"Look at you, stalking me online"
"I know, it's a bit creepy, but I was just checking on people's skills before I started getting people's hopes up. It isn't just you, it's Rob too."
"Rob? What are you up to?"
"Building a new business hopefully"
"Are you sure? Me and Rob working together?"
"You won't be working directly with Rob, you'll be more in charge of the business and administering everything"
"OK, but what is this then?"

"I'm still piecing it together, but I'm going to start an events company"

"What's that?" asked Hannah

"A company that arranges events for anyone. Corporate events, weddings, parties, anything like that."

"I've got no idea how to do any of that"

"You don't have to, I'm going to write plans and organise everything with you, then once it has been set up I will hand it over to you to run and keep going."

"Where does Rob fit in?"

"He is good with his hands, he loves practical work. I thought maybe he could dress the venues and if he suits up could help be an event rep."

"Wow, you have been thinking about this, haven't you?"

"Yeah, I really think it could work. I know how much you hate your current employer, I could give you a way out. I can give Rob a permanent job, a career for him. He desperately wants to settle down, it may have taken him longer than most, but I think he really wants to make something of himself."

"So just an excuse to create jobs for your mates?"

"No, I really think this business can work. If we do it right, it can be so successful. I look at the trouble I had with the reunion, I had to organise everything except the food. If only there was a company I could've contracted it to for a fixed fee, imagine how much easier my life could've been. Eventually we can get deals with venues and suppliers, start charging a package fee"

"Wow...you really are going for this aren't you?"

"Yes, I am. What do think?"

"You show me a plan, of how it will work and what makes it a viable business and I'll let you know"

"I thought you'd be easy to convince."

"I can't jump from my job, for some idea"

"I know, but you know I can make it work"

"I do, but I want you to prove it to me"

"I will keep working on it, I have financial teams working out the profit and figures we'd need to hit already"

"Good"
"Anyway, why are you here?"
"I told you I needed a friend"
"Why?"
"I got a letter"

Hannah showed James the letter that Paul had posted through the door.

"He sounds genuine" said James
"He sounds desperate" said Hannah
"What do you mean desperate?"
"He's lost his cushy life, when he was with me, he could freeload"
"I suppose"
"And he doesn't apologise for being lazy, cheap or not giving a toss. I've realised recently, he doesn't make me feel positive, I'm not in love with him and I'm not sure I ever was."
"What has brought this on, though? Surely not just his reaction at the reunion?"
"No, it is everything. I've been thinking about the past, he was an arsehole to me."
"Look, you've got a great group of friends, we'll support you. Me, Karen and even Rob at a push"
"Yeah I suppose"

Hannah smiled at James.

"Are you done with your plan for now?" said Hannah
"Well yes, there isn't much I can do until someone from the finance team gets back to me with the costings. Why?"
"Can I talk to you about school?"
"Of course you can"
"Was I really a bitch at school?"
"Only because Claire was oppressing you"
"I don't like the idea that people think that I was a cow"
"What has brought this on?"

"Karen's diary"
"You've read Karen's diary?"
"Only a little bit, she wanted me to read it. It had some comments about Rob in it."
"Was there anything about me?"
"No, but there was a comment about me being horrid to her"
"But that wasn't the real you"
"I know that, but I still did it."
"Karen doesn't care, she likes you."
"She does now, but she used to hate me"
"OK, what do you want me to say? Yes you were nasty to people, but you were in a difficult place. No one holds it against you, especially anyone who saw how you dealt with Claire the other night"
"I suppose, but how would I even begin to make it right for people that I did hurt?"
"I don't know, nationwide advert in a paper apologising to them?"
"Don't be daft"
"I'm not, if you want to apologise to lots of people, you've got think big"
"You think I've got that many to apologise to?"
"No, I think you are catastrophizing in your head. People won't care, and even if they do, you'll never know or see them again"
"I don't know, I just don't like people thinking bad of me"
"Like I've said, they've probably forgotten"
"I know, but seeing it written in black and white really hurt me"
"Look, Karen likes you and I like you. You were horrible to both of us at school. So don't worry"
"I suppose"
"Just don't dwell on it, no-one else will"
"Okay, thanks for chatting to me"
"No problem"
"I just needed a friend to listen to me. I didn't want to be in my house all alone tonight"
"Do you need a hug?"

"I can always do with one"

James held out his arms and hugged his friend close to him. She hugged him back tightly. James could feel her against himself and he could smell the scent of her hair. He loved this moment, he didn't want it to end, but he was becoming aware that this hug was starting to become uncomfortably long. He let go.

Hannah felt herself getting lost in the moment too, she loved the feeling of James holding her close, but she too was aware that this hug was held just a little too long.

"Thank you" said Hannah as they released each other
"You are always welcome" said James
"Look, I'm going to head off to bed in a second" said Hannah
"I'm heading off myself soon"
"Before I go, I'm going to get a hot chocolate, do you want one?"
"Yes, I think I will thanks"

CHAPTER 24

A Fun Day Out

Rob was up just before seven the following morning, this was early for him. He made sure he had plenty of time to get showered, dressed and have breakfast before the panic set in. He spent an hour making sure he had everything ready. Picnic, drinks, tickets. He wanted this day to be perfect. He kept checking and rechecking everything to make sure he hadn't forgotten anything at all. When it got to just after nine, he picked up his coat and headed for the door.

James had been up early too. He'd received an email from one of his finance guys saying that they had taken a quick look at the figures appeared to stack up for his new business. So now he needed to make proper plans. He hadn't even bothered to get dressed, he was sat in his boxer shorts at the little table in his bedroom tapping away at his laptop. He'd need an office, phone lines, internet presence, he'd want to hit the ground running. He'd sent emails out to local property agents, knowing full well they wouldn't let the weekend get in the way. It was just after nine when he got a message back from an agent with a list of offices available to rent in the area. He phoned the number on the bottom of the email.

"Hi, this is James Richardson, can I speak to Mike please?"
"This is Mike. You're keen aren't you, I've only just sent you the message"
"No time like the present Mike. I just wanted to say these are all

very nice, but do you have any to buy, rather than rent?"
"Sorry, I misunderstood. When you said you were starting a new business, I thought you'd want rental properties. I'll send you the relevant file over now."
"No, totally understand. What is availability like? I'd like to move quickly on this if I can"
"Some of these are available now, if you are interested in any of them, we can arrange viewing later today on most of them"
"Great, I'll be in touch once I've reviewed them"
"Thanks, bye"

James' laptop pinged as the email arrived. This idea had really got him excited. He wanted it to work and was sure it would. He had checked the local area online and no-one else was doing this sort of thing.

"James, are you up?" called Hannah from the hallway
"Yes, just looking at listings for potential offices" he called back

The bedroom door opened.

"You don't waste time do you?" said Hannah as she walked through the door. She looked up and realised James was sat there in his underwear.

"Sorry, I thought you were up" she said and closed the door again quickly.

"Don't panic, it's not like I'm naked" called James
"Oh, well I'll give you some time to get ready anyway" said Hannah from the other side of the door. "Do you want coffee or breakfast?"

"I'd love a coffee. We might have to go out for breakfast, we're getting a bit low on supplies." said James "Give me ten minutes to get ready and I'll come and show you my plans"
"No problem, I'll leave you to it"

Hannah went to make coffee, there was just enough milk for

them both to have one. Hannah stood there deep in thought, so many thoughts whirling around her head.

"Why doesn't my house seem like home?"
"Why do I feel comfortable here?"
"Why does James' place feel more like home than my own house?"
"Why do I feel I can tell James anything?"

"Is that my coffee?" asked James as he walked into the kitchen
"Err, what....yeah" said Hannah
"Sorry, did I interrupt your train of thought?"
"Yeah, kind of"
"Want to talk about it?"

Hannah burst into tears

"What's the matter?" asked James as he put his arm around her.
"I'm lost, I don't know what's going on, I'm so confused" sobbed Hannah
"What? Have I done something wrong? Can I help?"
"It's not you, not really"
"What is it?"
"I just don't know. My life has changed completely this week. I thought I had everything organised. I was engaged to someone, I had a house and a job that all though I didn't like it, at least I was reliable"
"I didn't realise that I'd upset your life so much"
"No, I don't mean that. I mean that everything has changed. I've lost Paul, and I know he's an arsehole and I don't want him back. I'm no longer happy at my house, it isn't my home. It has too many memories of Paul in it. As for my job, I wasn't happy, but when I left to look after you earlier this week, I might as well have told them to stick it. They haven't been in touch and I don't want to go back."
"Look, let's take these on, one at a time. As far as Paul goes, I can't help with that, I do know that you have friends who care for you."

"I know that too"
"Your house, don't worry about it. It will soon feel like a home"
"It won't, it wasn't ever my house, it was the house Paul wanted and I just took out the mortgage on it"
"Oh, well, if you don't want to spend time there, you are more than welcome to live here for now. I'm going to have to head back to the office on Monday, there is no reason you can't stay here. After all, you already have a key. We can work out what to do about your place when everything is a little more settled."
"Really? I don't want to impose"
"No, you are always welcome here, you know that. Now as far as your job goes, if my idea takes off, you won't need that job"
"I know, but I can't rely on you for everything"
"You're not relying on me, I believe in you. If you can't do the job, I can always fire you and get someone who can."
"Woah, I didn't say I can't do it"
"Good, then that's settled, anything else bothering you?"
"Just what I said last night about regrets."
"And I've already said not to worry about it"
"I suppose, so what is the plan?"
"I want you to come with me to look at some potential offices"
"Wow, you really are moving fast"
"I know, take a look at these ones that are available now"

James opened his laptop and started showing Hannah the property details that he'd been sent.

Rob arrived at Karen's house, got out of the car and walked up to the front door. He rang the doorbell and a squeal and the sound of running feet could be heard from behind the door. After a few seconds the door opened.

"Calm down" said Karen
"I can't I want to meet your friend" said Leo from behind the door
"OK then, Rob this is Leo" said Karen

Leo ran out from behind the door and stood slightly behind his mother's leg as he looked at the man in the doorway.

"Hello Leo" said Rob. No reply came from Leo
"Leo, say hello to Rob" said Karen
"He's very big" said Leo
"Sorry", said Karen to Rob, then she turned to Leo "Stop being silly and say hello to Rob"
"Hello Rob" said Leo
"Do we need anything with us today?"
"We're going to be outside, but the weather forecast is very good for today, so maybe some suncream?"
"Do you need a car seat?"
"Oh, sorry I hadn't thought about that, not that I have one anyway."
"That's fine, we'll get mine out of my car."
"Do we need to bring food or anything?"
"I have some food, if you want to bring yourself a drink or two, that'd probably be good"

Karen picked up a couple of drinks from the fridge and handed them to Rob. She then went to her car and got the car seat. She handed it to Rob who put it in the back of his car, carefully following the instructions on the side of the chair to fit it.

Karen and Leo came over to the car and Karen checked the seat was in properly.

"Very good, most people struggle with that the first time." said Karen
"Can I get in mummy?" asked Leo
"Yes, of course you can." replied Karen
Leo jumped in and Karen clipped his seatbelt in.
"Any clues to where we are going yet?" asked Karen as she got into the front seat. Rob got into the driver's seat and looked at Karen.
"I told you, it's a surprise. Here's a big clue though. Do you like

animals Leo?" said Rob
"Animals? Yeah!" replied Leo
"What have you got planned?" asked Karen
"No more clues. It sounds like he'll enjoy it" said Rob

Rob pulled away and drove off towards the end of town.

"Thank you for this, Leo has been looking forward to it since I told him we were going out for the day with a friend" said Karen
"That's fine, hopefully you guys will enjoy it." said Rob

Soon enough the road signs for the Zoo started to appear.

"I just saw an Elephant" said Leo from the backseat
"An Elephant, what a great imagination you've got Leo" said Karen
"I did mummy, it was on the sign" said Leo
"What sign?" said Karen
"The road sign" said Rob still trying not to give anything away.

A few minutes later they are driving down the road that passes the front of the Zoo. As they approach to entrance Rob slows down and indicates off of the main road.

"The Zoo?" said Karen
"Not just the Zoo" said Rob
"You are very mysterious" said Karen

They pull into the carpark and Rob, Karen and Leo get out of the car. Rob goes into the boot and grabs his drink and his little backpack. He takes note of the picnic area over towards the front entrance. They start walking towards the entrance.

"Sorry to say this Rob, but we're going to spend half the morning queuing by the look of it" said Karen
"No we won't" said Rob and continued walking towards the main door, totally ignoring the queue that stretched into the carpark and walking past everyone waiting.

"You can't just walk up to the front door" said Karen

"You can if you have these" said Rob and flashed three paper tickets that he was holding on to.
"You really have planned ahead haven't you?" said Karen

They reached the entrance and walked past the queues to a set of gates where staff were checking tickets. Rob held out the tickets to be checked. The man at the gate checked the tickets and then looked at Leo and asked "What's your favourite animal here?"

"He doesn't know" said Karen "He's never been here before"
"Then you are in for a treat and are very lucky. Don't forget to come to the office before you leave to get your picture taken and collect your cards" said the man on the gate
"Thanks" said Rob and they walked through the door.

Once they were past the entrance, Karen turned to Rob.

"Why do we need our picture taken?" asked Karen
"Oh, this isn't a one off" said Rob "These are annual tickets, we need to trade them in for little photo cards before the end of the day. I figured we'd probably want to come here more than once, and it is so big, you'd never do it all in one day anyway. Plus they have other stuff, like the play areas which I thought Leo might want to use at some point or another. Somewhere they even have a soft play centre with ball pits and slides, and a coffee area."
"It really sounds like you've got this all worked out" said Karen
"I have. I even have a picnic in the car" aid Rob "When we get hungry, we'll nip out to the picnic area out the front and I'll get everything from the boot of the car"
"Great!" said Karen
"What animals do you want to see first?" asked Rob to Leo
"Penguins! I love penguins" said Leo
"He does" said Karen with a nod.

Rob pulled a map out of his pocket.

The Reunion Of A Lifetime

"Penguins, ah, there they are" said Rob "Let's go this way then"
"Wait up..." said Karen as Rob and Leo dashed off towards some chimps enclosure "...you're going the wrong way!"

By the time Karen had caught up, they were looking at some chimps, Leo was being held up by Rob and so he could see better. Leo pressed his nose against the glass. A chimp in the enclosure was staring at Leo. Leo was laughing at the chimp and the chimp was clearly putting on a show for him.

Leo giggled as the chimp swung around on the ropes that were hanging down in the enclosure. Eventually the chimp stopped romping around and headed off towards another person. Rob put Leo back down on the floor.

"Did you see the monkey?" said Leo "He was laughing at me"
"You really shouldn't have run off like that" said Karen to Leo
"But I had Rob with me" said Leo "Rob is cool"
"Rob shouldn't have run off either" said Karen "What if I'd lost you guys, this place is huge"
"Sorry mummy" said Leo
"Sorry mum" said Rob cheekily with a grin
"It's alright, no harm done. But remember I care about you and don't want you getting lost. Stay with me, please" said Karen
"Okay" said Leo
"So where are the penguins then?" asked Rob
"You went completely the wrong way, here take a look at the map" said Karen

Karen opened out the map and pointed out how the penguins were in the opposite direction from the entrance.

Rob looked a little sheepish and said "I didn't really look at the map, I was looking at the pictures and the Penguin picture is just there". He pointed to a section to the right of the chimps enclosure on the map.
"That is just a photo of the animals, that is not part of the map"

said Karen "let's head this way, we can see the penguins and the meerkats this way", with that Karen took Leo's hand and walked off towards the penguin enclosure with Rob alongside.

"Do you think this is a good day out?" asked Rob
"Yes, I'm just a little nervous being out with all these other people. I don't want anything to happen to Leo" replied Karen
"We're both keeping an eye on him, it'll be fine" replied Rob
"I know, but we don't often go out to busy places. That is the beauty of working how I do, we can pop out during a weekday when everyone else is at school or work. So the saturday crush isn't something that happens to me that often, and certainly not when Leo is with me"
"Ah ok, sorry, my bad" said Rob
"Don't worry, I'm just not used to having someone else look out for Leo either" said Karen. They got to the penguins enclosure and Leo asked to be picked up for a better view, Rob obliged and held him against the glass looking at the penguins waddling around. Eventually Leo got bored of the penguins, they were having a break and sitting around.
"Do you want to look at the meerkats?" asked Karen "They're only along this path"
"Yay!" said Leo and grabbed Rob's hand. "I want to walk with Rob, can I?", he said
"Of course" said Karen. *"That's so cute"* she thought.

Rob seemed to be taking everything in his stride. He was so focused on having fun and looking at the animals that looking after Leo really didn't seem to have phased him. The truth was he was enjoying it, he loved the fact that Leo had taken to him and found the whole experience very rewarding. He was a natural at talking to Leo and he wasn't really even thinking about his relationship with Karen at this point. He figured they may have a chance to spend some time together later, but for now he was enjoying his time with Leo.

Karen couldn't be happier with the way the Leo was taking to

Rob. Rob seemed so confident with him, yet also caring. Leo was having a laugh, and holding hands with him. Leo seemed to trust him from the moment they'd met.

James and Hannah were out on their way to meet the property agent. Hannah was behind the wheel of her car driving to the business park on the edge of town. James sat there in the passenger seat looking through the particulars of the property. He was checking out details with his financial advisor on the phone as they drove. He'd managed to work out what his budget was and had a good idea of how much room he'd need to do this. They pulled into the car park of the newly built office.

"Oh my word" said Hannah
"What?"
"It's a huge building"
"I think you're looking at the wrong one" laughed James "Ours is over there"
"Oh, right" said Hannah

Hannah looked at the office on the other side of the car park.

"That looks much more like it" said Hannah

They walked up to the building. A man in a suit was waiting for them.
"Mr Richardson?" said the man
"Yes, are you Mike?" said James
"Yes I am." said the gentleman and he held his hand out to shake James'
"I am Hannah, Administrative manager" said Hannah and held her hand out.
"Oh, pleased to meet you" said Mike as he shook her hand. "Follow me please"

"Administrative manager?" whispered James to Hannah as they followed
"Easier than explaining our friendship again to someone" she

whispered back and smiled.
"Does that mean you've accepted the job offer?"
"Was I interviewed for it? I don't remember one"
"OK, I'll give you an interview when we get home" James said with a smile. Hannah grinned back at James. They turned a corner and walked up to the door.
"This is the entrance to the office" said Mike
"No shit" whispered Hannah to James
"Be serious a minute" said James
"Sorry" said Hannah "It's a nice entrance and hallway" she said to Mike
"It is, but you need to see the offices themselves" said Mike
"This is the reception area. The entire building has power and computer points throughout. There are 2 toilets to the left and a kitchenette to the right. The main offices are through here". Mike led them through a set of double doors into a large space. Big enough for six or seven generous working areas. James had seen offices of this size crammed with fourteen members of staff in them before.
"Nice space" said James.
"You haven't seen the managers' offices yet" said Mike
On the far side of the room there was a big glass partition, beyond which were three separate offices.

"I'm sure you have your own plans for them" said Mike as he crossed the room towards the offices "But we have three offices, so you can have a manager, supervisor and an HR office without them being in the main office."
"Interesting" said James
"I think we need to talk about this" said Hannah
"No, not at the moment anyway" whispered James
"These are really interesting offices. I mean there certainly is plenty of room in here, isn't there?" said James
"There certainly is. Do you need a copy of the particulars?" asked Mike
"It would be handy" said James

"Can I have a copy too?" asked Hannah

"Certainly" said Mike and dug out a couple of copies from his folder.

"What about car park and exterior?"

"All managed by the office over the other side. You effectively lease the car parking space from them, but they are ultimately responsible. All costs are in the file"

"I notice there are no radiators" said Hannah

"Overhead climate control units" said Mike "Controls by door and in each office allow you to set a temperature, heats when cold and runs air-conditioning when too warm, or a fan if you're worried about cost"

"Cool...or not as the case may be" said James with a grin.

"Well that's pretty much all there is to say" said Mike "The office upstairs is pretty much the same. Do you want to take a look?"

"Of course" said James

"Upstairs?" said Hannah

"I thought we could lease one of them out" said James

"If it's the same, I'll stay down here" said Hannah "I can visualise where everyone would be"

"OK" said Mike "we'll be back shortly". Hannah took some pictures of the office and went to the managers' offices at the back. *"I could imagine myself working in here"* she thought. Just then her phone sounded, a message from Karen..

"Rob has really come up trumps" said the message, a picture appeared of Rob holding Leo up at the side of the penguin's enclosure.

"Cute, are you at the zoo?" Hannah sent back

"Yes, he's paid for a special ticket for us to come whenever we like" came the response

"Wow, is he feeling flush?" sent Hannah

"Don't know, but he is definitely making an effort. He has lunch organised too apparently"

James and Mike reappeared in the office.

"Ready to go?" said James
"Yes" said Hannah
"I hope everything is to your satisfaction" said Mike as they walked out of the doors, "If you need any further information please let me know"
"Will do" said James

James and Hannah headed back to the car and got in, as they drove back to James' place, they chatted.

"What do you think?" asked James
"I could definitely work in that office, just needs some nice furniture" replied Hannah
"Good, I have an idea of someone who we could rent the other office out to" replied James
"Are we having the downstairs or upstairs office?" asked Hannah
"Downstairs, it'll be easier to move stock in and out of, if we need to"
"Good thinking" said Hannah
"So who is this for the other office?"
"I've already been online sounding out businesses in small premises about moving into a new office. I have two or three that are interested in cheaper office space. If I pitch it right we can make the office earn money for us"
"Us? This sounds interesting, how do I get my share of this money?" said Hannah
"You know what I mean, the business" said James with a smile.

Karen was really enjoying herself, they'd been around about a quarter of the zoo and it was just getting to lunchtime. Rob had been careful to ensure that they had made a loop and come back towards the entrance as it approached lunchtime.

"What are we doing back here?" said Karen
"We can get our pictures done and collect our passes, then nip out and have our lunch." replied Rob
"OK" said Karen. They went in the office and Rob went first, hav-

The Reunion Of A Lifetime

ing his picture taken, then a plastic card the same size and shape as a credit card was handed to him. It had his picture and some details on one side and the zoo logo on the other. Once Rob was done, Karen walked towards the counter.

Rob said "You deal with yours and Leo's and then come out the front to the tables. I'm going to sort our lunch". Rob went to the car and picked up his large cool-bag from the boot. He took it over to a table and started to unpack it. There were sandwiches, sausage rolls, crisps, cakes and other goodies.

Karen rounded the corner and she looked for Rob by the tables.

"Wow, that's a lot of food" she said as she walked over
"Cheese sandwiches!" said Leo
"I didn't know what you'd like" said Rob "So I bought a bit of everything. Anything we can't eat, you can take home."
"Cheese sandwiches" said Leo again
"Yes there are cheese sandwiches" said Rob
"You are amazing" said Karen with a smile. She lent over and gave Rob a peck on the cheek
"Oooo, kissy kissy" said Leo. Rob went red, Karen looked a little sheepish.
"It was a thank you kiss" Karen said to Leo, she winked to Rob, "we both owe Rob a big thank you for today"
"Thank you" said Leo and he walked over and hugged Rob. Karen looked at Rob and Leo and smiled.

They sat and ate food and discussed animals to see that afternoon.
"Eflehunts" said Leo
"It's elephants" said Rob
"He always says Eflehunts" said Karen
"Eflehunts" repeated Leo with a grin
"Do they have elephants?" asked Karen
"There's a picture there" said Leo, pointing to the map on the side of the building.

"OK, we'll look at the elephants. What else?" asked Rob
"Giraffes" said Leo
"OK, Giraffes, anything you would like to see?" Rob asked Karen
"Hmmm, do they have any tigers?" replied Karen
"Yay, tigers" said Leo
"I'm sure they do" said Rob.
"They're near the giraffes" said Leo still pointing at the map.
"You are very observant" said Rob
"What does that mean?" asked Leo
"It means you look around and see information that others miss" said Karen.
"Is everyone done?" asked Rob
"Yes, I think we are" said Karen
"Can I have a cake?" said Leo
"Alright" said Rob. Leo took a cake from the tray. Rob then packed everything back up in the cool-bag and took it back to the car.
"OK" said Rob, let's go then. Have you both got your cards?
"I've got them both" said Karen "I wouldn't give Leo his in case he lost it. I told him it is worth a lot of money and mustn't get lost". Leo looked at Karen and smiled.
"Let's go then" said Rob and led them both back into the Zoo.

They spent the afternoon looking at animals, Rob even bought them all ice creams as they went around. They eventually had to stop at around four o'clock as Leo was getting worn out. They headed back towards the entrance, they passed through the gift shop and Leo wanted to look at the toys.

"You aren't having anything" said Karen "Rob has been kind enough to buy us tickets that mean we can come back whenever we want"
"Can we come back tomorrow?" asked Leo
"No, we can't. We have to go to Grandma's tomorrow" replied Karen
"What about the day after?" challenged Leo

"Maybe you and I could come back on Monday, if I get all of my work done." replied Karen

"What about Rob?" asked Leo

"I'm sure Rob is busy" replied Karen

"We'll have to see but I'm trying to get a new job at the moment." said Rob

"It's not fair" said Leo "I want Rob to come with us"

"I will, when I can" said Rob "But for now, we need to get you home"

"I like penguins" said Leo

"I know you do, but we're not getting you a toy today" said Rob "Maybe if you are good for mummy, I'll let you have one next time we all come together"

"Yay!" shouted Leo

"Come on let's get you guys home" said Rob

"Thanks" whispered Karen "I thought he was going to have a meltdown if he didn't get a toy"

"I know my stuff" said Rob with a wink.

CHAPTER 25

An Evening Together

"Right" said Rob as the car pulled up outside Karen's "Back home safe and sound"
"Sound is right", said Karen and pointed to the back seat where Leo was fast asleep in his car-seat.
"Bless" said Rob
"Would you mind carrying him in?" asked Karen
"No, that's fine" said Rob

Karen and Rob got out of the car and Rob walked around to the back door of the car and opened it. Leo was still sound asleep. Rob undid the seatbelt, reached across and lifted Leo out of his seat. As Rob carried him from the car, Leo began to stir, looked around saw Rob was holding him, smiled and closed his eyes and hugged into him. Karen beamed at Rob, Rob smiled back. He was feeling so natural with Leo. Yes, Leo was four and inquisitive about everything and it was hard work looking after Leo, even just for a short while, but Rob was in his element.

Rob took Leo into the living room and put him down gently on the sofa. As he did Leo woke up immediately.

"We didn't see the Lemurs" he said
"We'll go and see them next time" said Rob
"Thank you" said Leo
"Are you guys hungry? We've still got loads of food left over" said Rob
"That's a good idea" said Karen

"Zoo food?" asked Leo

"Yes, the food we had at the zoo" replied Rob

"OK" said Leo. Karen leant over to Rob and whispered in his ear. "Wow, you get a thank you unprompted and no arguments about having the same food for tea as lunch. Someone's doing something right" she said

"I'll be back in a minute" said Rob "I've just got to get the stuff from the car". He wandered out the door and got the cool-bag out of the car boot. He brought the bag in and went through to the kitchen. He unpacked everything on the little dining table. They really did still have loads of food, certainly enough for a reasonable evening meal each.

"Dinner is served" Rob called out. Leo came hurtling through the door just a few seconds later making a noise like a racing car. He made a skidding sound and stopped next to the table.

"Oh my word" said Karen, "I can't believe how much food we still have"

"Cheese sandwich?" asked Leo

"I'm sure you can have a cheese sandwich" said Rob "But maybe you'd like something different as well. Sausage rolls or little pizzas?"

"Cheese sandwich" said Leo with a nod

"Here's a cheese sandwich" said Karen "Now if you want you can have something else afterwards"

"Having a load of picnic type food always reminds me of what I used to do when I was a kid" said Rob

"Oh yeah, what was that?" asked Karen

"Put weird combinations of food together. Like a cheese sandwich with party sized sausage rolls in the middle of it, or crisps in sandwiches or on top of quiches" replied Rob

"Don't" said Karen "I don't want Leo getting silly ideas". Rob and Karen turned to look at Leo who was at that very moment putting a handful of crisps in between the slices of bread, and looking very pleased with himself.

"Sorry" said Rob. Karen smiled and looked at the two of them.

As Rob now joined in making his own crisp sandwiches.

They all sat and ate their food, by the time they were finished, there were just a few sausage rolls left.

"Can I go and play mummy?" asked Leo
"Of course you can. But we do need to give you a bath soon, you smell like the zoo" replied Karen
"OK" said Leo "Rob, do you want to play?"
"Let's go" said Rob and the pair of them got up from the table and headed for the living room.

Karen looked at the pair of them as they walked into the living room, she was stunned by how well Leo had taken to Rob. It was so rare for him to even invite her to play games with him, normally she'd have to coax Leo into playing with her. Yet here he was engaging and encouraging Rob to join in.

Karen left them playing and cleared up the food in the kitchen. It was as she walked back through, she realised that this was an important moment for her. She'd left Leo with Rob and trusted Rob completely to keep him safe. Yes she'd left James with Leo the other day, but this was different. With James, they were watching TV and she was keeping an ear out. With Rob, she really had let go and wasn't even paying attention to what was going on.

She watched them playing together, both with the building bricks making different things. Leo was building a house, Rob had got a handful of wheels and was building a car.

"What is it?" asked Leo
"A car" said Rob
"It has too many wheels" said Leo
"Do you think ten wheels is too much?" asked Rob
"Yes silly, cars have four wheels" replied Leo
"Won't it go faster with more wheels?" asked Rob
"Ahem" said Karen, "I hate to break up this conversation, but we

The Reunion Of A Lifetime

need to get you bathed and ready for bed little boy"
"Aw" said Leo
"You can see Rob again, I'm sure he won't mind playing another day"
"Is that my queue to go?" asked Rob
"If you want to" said Karen "or you can watch TV whilst I get Leo bathed and off to bed and then we can have some time together"
"OK" said Rob, he turned to Leo "Look mate, I've had good fun today and I hope you have too"
"It's been great" said Leo
"I'll see you soon" Rob said to Leo as Karen picked him up
"See you" said Leo as Karen carried him out of the room and up the stairs. Rob tidied up the blocks back into their box, leaving their constructions complete on top of it. He wandered into the living room, sat down on the sofa and turned on the TV.

About half an hour later, Karen called down the stairs
"Rob, can you come here a second?" she yelled
"OK"
Rob got up from the sofa where he'd been watching some quiz show that was on the TV and walked to the bottom of the stairs.

"What is it?" he shouted up the stairs
"Can you come up?" asked Karen
When Rob got to the top of the stairs he could see the light on in a room off to one side of the landing, he walked over to the doorway, this was clearly Leo's room.

"Someone wanted to say goodnight" said Karen.

Leo was sat on his bed in his pyjamas smiling. He had a book in his hand.

"Can you read me a story?" asked Leo holding out his book.

Rob walked over to the bed and accepted the book from Leo. Rob sat down next to the bed and began to read as Karen watched on. The story was quite short and over in around five minutes, but Rob had given all the characters voices and done actions as he read. Leo had listened attentively throughout, despite it being a story he'd heard lots of times before.

"Thank you", said Leo "You read stories well"
"No, thank you for listening. I hope you've had a good time today, but it is time to get off to sleep now"
"Night night" said Leo and reached out his arms for a hug
"Night night" said Rob and lent in and hugged him tightly.
"I'll see you in a minute" Rob said to Karen and left the room, he stayed just out of sight of the bed in the hallway and listened.
"Mummy" said Leo
"Yes, dear" replied Karen
"I like Rob"
"I know you do"
"I think he's going to be my best friend"
"You're so sweet, it's time to sleep now"
"Night night, mummy"
"Night night, little Leo" said Karen "Sweet dreams"
"I'll dream of sweets" said Leo
"Yes you will" said Karen and hugged and kissed the little boy.

Karen walked out into the hallway where Rob was waiting.

"Be quiet, let's get downstairs" she whispered to Rob

They headed off down the stairs and back into the living room. They sat down next to each other on the sofa.

"You tidied up the toys?" asked Karen
"Of course" replied Rob
"You're so sweet. Thank you for today, you've been wonderful"
"It has been a pleasure. I've really enjoyed every moment"
"You really have surprised me. You seem to take Leo completely in your stride"
"I don't know what it is. I just feel so comfortable around you and him and I feel more confident in myself than I have done in a long time. I feel like I finally have a purpose and direction"

"Really? Any idea why?"

"Not really, I just really want to make a success of myself, and I find being with you and Leo easy. It helps that Leo is such a good kid"

"You haven't seen the worst of him yet, wait till he tantrums with you"

"When that happens I'm sure I'll deal with it"

"You sure?"

"Look I really am enjoying my time with you guys, and do you know what? I know it's early days for us, but I really do think that I…"

"Be sure before you say it" said Karen "Because I think if you say it, I'll say it too and then if it doesn't work out I'm going to be a broken person"

"No pressure then" said Rob

"Sorry, but I didn't want you saying something you didn't mean. That word has such power and at the moment my feelings for you are so strong, but I don't want to say it unless we both mean it."

"OK, I totally understand." Rob said and then paused. Eventually he took Karen's hand in his and looked her straight in the eyes.

"Karen Jennings, I have known you since school and I never would have dreamt that you would give me a chance to spend time with you. Let alone let me into your life the way that you have the last few days. You are wonderful, caring, honest and open with me, your son is a credit to you and I want to be part of that life. I know I'm not much of a catch, but I am trying to turn my life around and it is you that is driving me to do that. Karen Jennings, I think…well I know, I love you"

There it was, those three words hanging in the air.

Karen stared deep into Rob's eyes and replied "I think I'm in love with you too"

The two embraced and kissed, their first real kiss as a couple.

CHAPTER 26

Putting Plans In Motion

It was just gone ten on Sunday morning when Rob's phone rang. Rob tapped the screen to answer the call.

"Hi Rob" said James
"Hi" said Rob
"Well?" said James
"Well, what?" said Rob
"Well, how did your trip out go?"
"Great actually, we had a wonderful day"
"Great to hear."
"Look, I'm just bursting to tell someone"
"What"
"Me and Karen are going to give it a go."
"Give what a go?"
"Being a couple, we sat down and talked about our real feelings last night and we kissed and cuddled for ages on the sofa"
"That's great news, mate" said James
"Is that Rob?" shouted Hannah across the room at James
"Yeah" said James
"How did yesterday go?" asked Hannah
"I think it went well, I'll tell you in a bit. I need to talk to Rob about everything we've got planned"
"Oh yeah of course, I'll leave you to it" said Hannah
"What plan?" asked Rob down the phone
"I've got a business proposition for you"
"For me?" asked Rob

"Yes, for you"

"What is it then?"

"I am setting up a new company putting on events and I want you to join. Initially as an account manager"

"Account manager, that sounds like a cool job. It sounds really important."

"It's probably going to be a lot of hard work, especially to start with."

"I don't mind."

"To start with you're probably going to have to do everything, from client liaison to organising events and even actually putting decorations up for the event"

"Am I going to get paid for it?"

"Of course, I'll put you on a salary. I'll work out the specifics, but it'll probably be more than you've ever earned"

"Wow, really?"

"Yes, really. Hannah is going to work for the company too. She'll be the day to day manager."

"You mean I am going to be working for Hannah?"

"No you'll be working for me, Hannah is just going to make sure everything is running smoothly"

"It sounds great. Thank you"

"I have put in place the paperwork to get us an office to work from and setup the company name"

"Wow"

"I will be in touch once everything is in place."

"Cool"

After James had hung up the phone he went to find Hannah in the living room.

"So how was your call?" asked Hannah

"It went well. Rob certainly seems onboard" replied James

"Great. How does he feel about working for me?"

"He did ask about it. I told him that he'd be working for me, but you'd be making sure everything runs smoothly"

"So I'm not in charge?"
"Of course you are, I just wanted to get him onboard before I drop that bombshell on him fully"
"He'll be pissed off when he realises"
"No he won't, I'll explain it to him. Obviously you are better experienced in that sort of job role and he'll have to accept it."
"OK. Did he say anything about how yesterday went"
"Really well, I think him and Karen are an item"
"Oh, how sweet. I take it he got on well with Leo?"
"I think so, why don't you call Karen?"
"I will do shortly. Are we still on for an afternoon in the pub?"
"The pub?"
"Yes, we need to go back to our mystery couple"
"Oh…the guy and his bit on the side?"
"Exactly"
"OK, pub meal out this afternoon then?"
"Definitely" said Hannah with a smile "I'm going to go and call Karen". Hannah walked into her room and picked up her phone.

"Hi Karen"
"Hi, calling for gossip?"
"What do you take me for?"
"Someone who likes a bit of gossip"
"OK, you got me. So tell me then"
"What about?"
"About you and Rob and yesterday"
"Oh that!"
"Of course that!"
"I know, I'm pulling your leg. It was nice, we had a good time. Rob and Leo got on well together and it was lovely."
"And?"
"And what?"
"And, what else?"
"We had a wonderful day, he made lunch which we also had for dinner too as there was so much. He helped read Leo a bedtime story. It was great"

"And then what?"

"We had a conversation, and a moment, and I think we're going out"

Hannah squealed down the phone

"I'm so pleased for you" said Hannah

"I am too, I've been on cloud nine all morning" said Karen "Leo has been busy this morning drawing in his diary. He has drawn a picture of him, me and Rob at the zoo.

"Wow, how was Rob with Leo?"

"He was wonderful, he has taken to it so naturally. I'm still worried that Rob has no real direction in his life and is not earning money"

"He will be, he's just been offered a full time job that should lead to a career"

"He has? Where did you hear that?"

"James just offered it to him"

"But James' company is miles away"

"Not working for that company, the new one that I'm going to be managing"

"Oh, what company is this?"

"An events company. We've bought an office and everything, well I think we have, James has all of it in hand apparently. We are going to be a contractor that you call for when you want corporate events or things like weddings or anything like that"

"Oh my word. So when did this happen?"

"James dropped it on me the other night. I think it's a great idea. It came to him because of all the hassle he had organising the reunion. He thought why isn't there a company you can pay to do this for you in the local area? And now there is going to be"

"Amazing" said Karen "So when do you start?"

"Whenever I like, I just need to hand my notice in at my old job and work out my notice period"

"Jeez. I take it nothing further has been heard of from Paul?"

"No, nor Claire"

"Hmmm, I thought Paul might try harder. If you've been together that long, I don't know why he wouldn't"

"Because I made it quite clear I don't care about him and don't want him back"
"I suppose, but I thought he'd try harder" said Karen
"He's a spinless prat"
"Do you know if he's hanging around with Claire?"
"No idea, I don't care. I've moved on"
"Oh got your eye on someone have you?"
"Maybe, but I'm not sure I'm ready yet."
"Do tell"
"I'm not telling you, not yet"
"Spoil sport!"
"I know, sorry" said Hannah "Look, I'll give you call later, maybe you can come and meet me and James, we're going out for the afternoon to the old mill."
"Do you know if kids are allowed there?"
"I think so. I will check and let you know"
"OK, great, maybe I'll see you later"
"OK, bye"

Hannah walked back into the living room.

"I think Karen might meet us later" she said to James
"Oh, great" said James "Here, look at this"
"What is it?"
"It is the plan that I used to organise the reunion"
"Wow, that's a lot of tasks"
"I know, that's what we're going to take on"
"But this is just the reunion"
"Yes, and it didn't include organising catering, the school did that for us"
"Can we do this?"
"Let's try, shall we?"

James and Hannah spent the rest of the morning drawing up plans for different events. They spent time working out exactly what was a requirement, what they could offer as optional items and what the approximate lead times would be for them.

"Right, where are we now" asked James
"We have plans for weddings, engagements, anniversaries and reunions of course"
"That seems like a good start"
"It is a start, but we need to nail big birthday parties and the like too"
"Good idea, maybe we'll tackle it later"
"Later?"
"Yeah, I'm getting hungry, and time is getting on. We should get ourselves sorted and go for our afternoon out."
"Oh yeah"

Hannah and James got themselves ready and James called them a taxi.

CHAPTER 27

A Question Of Trust

As they got in the taxi, James got his phone out.

"Are you ready for this Shelly?" he said
"Shelly?"
"Yes, you're Shelly, I'm Peter" said James
"Oh yeah, good job you said something. I'd totally forgotten"

When they arrived, James led Hannah around the outside of the building and opened a side door to the bar.

"Why are we going this way?" asked Hannah
"Because this way we have to walk right past the whole bar"

They walked into the bar and their target couple were already sat at the bar. Caitlin holding on to her partner's hand and laughing and joking. Hannah walked past Caitlin and smiled at her as she made her way to a table. James stood next to the mystery man and got the bartender's attention. James ordered their drinks and they went and sat at a table.

Caitlin was laughing and joking with the man whilst James had stood at the bar. Once James was sat down at the table he exchanged glances with the guy at the bar. He nodded at James in acknowledgement of him.

"How are we going to play this?" asked Hannah
"Already way ahead of you" said James, he flashed something from his pocket at Hannah

The Reunion Of A Lifetime

"What is that?" she asked
"A mobile phone, it was just laying there on the bar"
"You are so sneaky"
"Do you know what you want to eat?"
"Not yet"
"Well make up your mind, I'll be back in a minute"
"What are you up to?"
"Just leave me to it and make sure you know what you want. I haven't got much time"
"OK"

James nipped off out to the lobby. A few minutes later he came back looking pleased with himself. Hannah put her phone away as he returned and gave James her order for food. James returned to the bar and placed the order.

"Excuse me" James said to the man at the bar
"Oh, Hi, Peter isn't it?"
"Yes, good memory"
"Can I help you?"
"More can I help you. You nearly knocked this phone off of the bar. Is it yours?"
"Oh, thanks, you would not know how many times I've left my phone on the bar here"
"Something distracting you?"
"Yeah something like that"
"Well never mind, you've got it now"
"Thanks again"

James returned to his table and sat down with Hannah

"What are you playing at?"
"In good time, I reckon about quarter of an hour max and you'll know what I'm up to"
"Mmmm, not sure I like it. Whatever it is"
"Oh, I just decided the direct approach was better" said James with a wink "Anyway, until then do you want to discuss other

ideas for the company?"
"Well I was thinking about big things, you know like hot air balloon rides and that sort of thing"
"That sounds great, any idea how that would work?"
"None at all yet"

Hannah and James continued to discuss their new business opportunities whilst they waited for their food. Hannah clearly trying to think outside of the box and make the company a real talking point. She knew exactly what the business needed.

James and Hannah were sat at their table and waiting for their food when an all too familiar voice was heard from just out of sight at the end of the bar.

"Right I'm here, what do you need?" asked the woman
"Honey" said the man at the bar as he spun around "What are you doing here?"
"Answering your fucking message, my darling" the woman walked along the front of the bar towards the man and came into view of James and Hannah. Claire stood there looking at the man with a look of thunder on her face.

"Getting a friend to call me to the bar, saying something was wrong and I had to get here as soon as I can" said Claire
"I have no idea what you are talking about"
"Nick, who is this?" asked Caitlin
"Yes Nick, why don't you explain to her who I am? Or should I say Steve?" said Claire
"Caitlin, this is Claire. Claire is my wife"
"Wife?"
"Oh, he didn't tell you, just like he didn't tell you his real name?"
"No"
"Sodding typical"
"Claire, we can talk about this"

Claire picked up Steve's pint from the bar and threw it across his shirt.

"Of course we can. I'll get a lawyer on to it first thing tomorrow"
"OK, I deserved that" said Steve

Caitlin picked up her drink and emptied it over Steve's head from behind

"You lying prick" she said as he spun around

As Steve was reeling from this Caitlin pulled his bar stool out from under him and he hit the floor.

"Don't call me" she said and stormed away from him and headed for the door.

"Sorry" she whispered in Hannah's direction

It was then that Claire caught sight of them. Hannah and James sat in the corner of the bar staring at everything unfolding in front of them.

"Oh, I knew you'd be in on it, you bitch" said Claire to Hannah
"What?" said Hannah
"How long have you known my husband was having an affair?"
"I didn't" said Hannah
"So you expect me to accept that you just happened to be here? After all, the young slut obviously knows you"
"Now wait a minute. We were here last week and got talking that was all. I had no idea you were involved in this or what was going on"
"Don't give me that, you've set it up haven't you? It wouldn't surprise me if you introduced them to each other. After all that's what you've always wanted, to get one up on me"
"Now hang on!" yelled James
"Oh, yes the prat is here too"
"Fucking shut up Claire. We'd never even met them until last week. We bumped into them here after Hannah called me when she'd kicked Paul out for sleeping with you"
"Woah, I never slept with Paul" said Claire

"Paul said that too, but I don't care" said Hannah

"You are a sad excuse for a friend Hannah. You never were up to much, you'll never be a success, you'll never be able to match up to me, and you know it."

"Right, I've had enough of your shit Claire" said James "Hannah here is twice the woman, or more than you'll ever be. She is the most kind and considerate, and the loveliest person I have ever met. She thinks of everyone else first. She is spectacular in a way you could never be. She is the most important person in my world. She had no idea you were involved. Neither did I, even when I made the call"

"You called her?" asked Steve

"You left your phone on the bar, I just called home for you"

"Well then, if that's true then I suppose I have to thank you James" said Claire "But just so we're clear, this doesn't make us friends"

"I wouldn't want to be friends with you" said James

"Neither would I" said Hannah with a smile

"You'll be hearing from my lawyer" Claire said to Steve and then stormed back out the door.

Steve was still stood there drenched in beer and gin, a little overwhelmed at what had just happened.

"Why?" said Steve

"Why what?" said James

"Why did you do it? I thought we were getting on."

"Hey, I don't like people who lie and cheat"

"But we're mates. You broke the unwritten rules. You're a sneaky slimy guy with no backbone"

"Excuse me…" said James

"I've got this" interrupted Hannah "You, are a low life cheating bastard. Whereas this man has integrity, honesty and really cares for people. I would trust this man with my life, I don't think there is anyone that would say that about you."

"Fuck you" said Steve

"Give it a rest will you" said the bartender to Steve "It is quite clear that you are the cause of the trouble here, I want you out now."
"But" said Steve
"No, out now, or I call the police" said the bartender.

Steve walked towards the door.

"Arseholes!" he shouted back into the bar as he left.

"Well that all got a bit intense, didn't it?" said Hannah
"Just a little" said James
"Did you really know Claire was involved?"
"No, not at all. Even when I was on the phone, I didn't realise it was her I was talking to"
"Small world though, eh?"

Just then James' phone rang

"Hello?" said James
"Hi Mr Richardson, Inspector Davis here"
"What can I do for you Inspector?"
"Just a quick update to say that we've charged a gentleman with the assault on you. I have to ask, do you know a Paul Taylor?"
"Paul?"
"You do know him?"
"Kind of"
"Well he has been given a conditional bail to avoid contact with yourself or Hannah Waters"
"OK, do you need anything from me?"
"Not at all"
"OK, then if that is everything, I'll say good evening"
"Certainly sir, good evening"

CHAPTER 28

True Friends

"Paul has been charged with the attack on me" said James
"Paul?" said Hannah
"Yeah, who guessed?"
"So that's why he was all apologetic in that letter"
"Oh, does that change anything?"
"No I still think he's a prat" said Hannah "Anyway, I'm still thinking about what you said earlier"
"What's that"
"I believe it was something like I'm kind and considerate and lovely and more than twice the woman Claire would ever be."
"Oh and what about what you said?"
"What did I say?"
"I think it was integrity and honesty and you'd trust me with your life."
"I would"
"I would trust you with mine too" said James "Hannah, I've known you all my life. You were there at every milestone in my childhood. You were my best friend through primary school. I trust you completely."
"I guess I feel the same way. We're so connected, we're on the same wavelength, we even have a similar sense of humour." said Hannah

Hannah stared at James' lips as he responded

"Hannah, I feel I need to say something." said James "The truth is, I know we've only really spent a week together after all those years, but I can't live without you. I love you, Hannah Waters"

Hannah felt the words that followed flow out of her mouth, no thought required. She said "James Richardson, my first friend, my best friend. You are my soulmate, the person I live for. I love you so much"

Hannah leant across the table and kissed James, James kissed her back. As they finished their first kiss, Hannah settled back into her chair and someone coughed to her side.

"Your food madam" said the member of staff
"Oh thank you" said Hannah
"I'm sorry, I didn't want to interrupt" said the staff member
"It's fine, thank you" said James

Hannah and James smiled at each other. Their worlds had changed in an instant. James looked deep into Hannah's eyes.

"I've never noticed that before" said James
"What?" asked Hannah
"Your eyes, when the light hits them right, I can see little flecks of green in them"
"You're so sweet" said Hannah
"Can I ask you something else?" asked James
"What?"
"Can I kiss you again?"
"Of course"

Hannah moved her chair around to the side of the table so they were now sat next to each other instead of opposite and they exchanged another kiss.

"Your food will get cold" came a familiar voice that broke the silence
"Rob? What are you doing here?" said James
"Came for an afternoon out with the family, if you don't mind" said Rob

There stood behind Rob was Karen and Leo.

"So when did this interesting development happen?" asked Karen
"About five minutes ago" said Hannah
"It should've happened years ago" said James
"So are we all happy families?" asked Karen
"It looks that way" replied Hannah
"It sounds like a cause for celebration" said Rob, "So are you getting a round in James?"

THE END

CHAPTER 29

A Sneak Peak: What The Future Holds

SIX MONTHS LATER

Hannah sat at her desk in her smart new office looking at the nameplate on the door.

"Assistant Director" she said out loud "Assistant, Director"
"Don't you forget it", said James as he rounded the corner
"Forget what?" said Hannah
"Assistant Director" said James "Emphasis on the assistant, you need to assist your director"
"But that's you" she said
"Of course, who else would you assist?"
"You said I could run this business"
"You can, I'm only director in name really, it's your business to oversee"
"Good, so you won't be needing the other office then?"
"Of course I will. I need somewhere to sleep when it all gets too much upstairs"
"Oh yeah, what is going on with upstairs. You said you had someone to rent it"
"And I do. It is my new sales office for my company"
"So what does that mean?"
"In real terms, I have two offices in the same building, one upstairs and one downstairs" James grinned

"And you'll do bugger all work in either of them" said Hannah

"Nothing changes there then!" shouted Rob from the other side of the open plan office. He'd got a desk all setup with a computer on it and was sat on a swivel chair spinning around.

"There's something missing" he said and pulled a picture of Karen and Leo out of his desk drawer and stood it on the desk next to a computer screen.

"Can someone help me with this?" said Karen. She was holding a large cardboard box which was trying to wedge itself in between the main office doors.

"Hi babe, what's in there?" asked Rob
"A selection of helium balloons" replied Karen
"Where do you want these balloons?" called Rob to James
"It's not like we're short of space, just put them anywhere out of the way for now." replied James
"Hi Karen" said Hannah
"Hi Mrs Boss" said Karen
"Now you know I'm not your boss" said Hannah "I'm a customer and you are a supplier"
"I still don't see why I can't be the boss" said Rob
"You need to work your way up" said James "I've yet to see you produce anything productive on that computer"
"Fair enough" said Rob

At that moment the phone on Rob's desk rang.

"The publicity must've started going out" said Hannah
"First advert on the local radio this morning" said James "Anyway, I must get on upstairs"

James headed out the door as Rob answered the phone.

"Hi, Rediscovered Events, you're speaking to Rob. How can I help you?" said Rob down the phone
"My, he sounds professional" said Karen

"This has taken a day of training to get him to this level." said Hannah

"But you know he'll be great with the customers" said Karen

"I know, but we need to make sure he's professional" replied Hannah

"Oh, he has done nothing but worry about being professional all week" said Karen "I think he really has turned a corner"

"I know, it's lovely to see. How are you two getting on since he moved in?"

"He's wonderful, he cooks, cleans, looks after Leo. Totally not the person I thought he'd be from way he used to act"

"I know"

"How are things with you and the boss in the mansion?"

"Fabulous, I even have a little news for you. I spoke to James this morning and I don't want to say anything until we've done a test, but I think I may be pregnant."

TO BE CONTINUED...

ABOUT THE AUTHOR

Surprisingly to most, I am a man who has always been in love with the story of love. My favourite films are all romantic comedies, this is where it started for me.

However, a few years ago, I started reading more and found that I fell in love with romantic novels, much more than the films I was used to. Suddenly you had an insight into thoughts and feelings that you couldn't get in a film. A book would take me a few weeks to read just a chapter every evening but I became totally invested in the characters' lives.

After a recent period of depression in my life, I decided to try something, and I started writing. It flowed so easily from my fingers and my mind knew exactly where it wanted the story to go.

I initially intended to release this book under my own name, but finding very few romantic comedy style novels written by men I decided to create myself a pen name, and hence Carolyn Kemp was born.

Printed in Poland
by Amazon Fulfillment
Poland Sp. z o.o., Wrocław